So I Accidentally became an Alien Outlaw's Mate

Sophia Sebell

CONTENTS

CHAPTER ONE
ABIGAIL

"Your man's back," Harris whispered.

I set the crate of bananas on the ground and glanced over my shoulder. There wasn't really a need to look. I knew exactly who he was talking about. My admirer dipped his head to avoid hitting the doorway as he stepped through the automatic door. He was wearing the same thing he always did, even in the heat of summer, a black duster coat, gloves, boots, a red scarf and a hat pulled down, with only a slit visible that his eyes peered from.

While he never did anything necessarily scary, he gave me the creeps. I'd never caught him doing it, but my co-workers frequently told me he'd leer at me when I wasn't looking. Plus, he never spoke. Twice a month, like clockwork, he'd come into the store and buy every single banana we had. Even stranger, he'd disappear into the woods behind the store with them.

"Well, he's in for a treat this time," I said. "Do you think he'll actually buy all these?"

"I'm sure Lauren would be hyped for that. She was stressing about accidentally ordering so many shipments of bananas," Harris replied, still staring at the man as he carefully maneuvered around some shopping carts, keeping his distance from them.

"Do you think he eats all of them? Is that all he eats?"

Harris shrugged. "Who knows? Maybe he's got a fetish?"

I giggled. "Maybe."

Harris stared back at the doorway and his eyes went wide as a shadow crossed over me. Quickly stepping out of the way, I motioned towards the massive display of bananas we had just put together. It was a little irritating. We had spent the last two hours organizing this display to get people to buy our surplus, and now he was probably going to clean us out before anyone saw it. I had even made a little banana person.

The man towered over me, his massive frame taking up far too much space for a normal person. I always wondered if he was some celebrity bodybuilder that tried to stay incognito while he shopped. *Maybe the secret to getting buff was just eating a lot of bananas?* The way his duster hugged him made it seem unlikely that he was just over-weight.

His eyes locked with mine, piercing ice set in sunburned skin. I had noticed the red skin around his eyes before. It didn't make sense how he even got sunburned if he was always covered head to toe and did his shopping at two in the morning. His gaze shifted to the pile of bananas and his eyes went wide behind the scarf.

"Yeah, we accidentally ordered too many," I offered as he pulled out a small notebook and scribbled in it before pulling out a large wad of cash. I stole a peek at what he was writing and saw lots of numbers as he calculated the cost of the bananas.

"How many pound?" a soothing, deep voice asked from the man's direction.

I glanced around him, looking for someone else behind his bulky frame, but realized it was his voice. He had been coming here for a year now and this was the first time that he actually spoke.

His eyes fell on me again, and his head tilted slightly as I stared at him blankly.

"Oh… um, Harris?" I wasn't completely sure what the weight would be. Harris was the one that accepted the deliveries.

Harris fidgeted with his blue apron while he mumbled under his breath, trying to add up the total weight. *Susie is going to be pissed if she has to ring all this up.* I grinned at myself. Susie was one of the overnight cashiers and kind of a jerk, so I hoped he would buy them all. Kyra just left on her lunch and Susie would get stuck with the check-out. It would take her hours to weigh and ring these up. There had to be easily two thousand of them.

The man bent over and peeked into the crates we hadn't unloaded yet while Harris tried to figure out the total. His back straightened immediately, and he went on high alert, dipping a hand into his coat, as a shopping cart rattled down an aisle towards us. A small elderly woman in a floral dress slowly moved past, being side-eyed the entire time by him. Once she was out of sight, he relaxed and resumed looking over the bananas.

"Are you okay?" I asked, unable to help myself. He had always acted oddly and seemed almost scared of the shopping carts. Now that he was speaking, I wanted to try for some answers.

He didn't respond or acknowledge me, just stared at Harris.

"Roughly a thousand pounds," Harris finally said.

"How many bananas?" the man asked.

"Maybe three thousand? Somewhere around there."

"I will purchase." He extended his hand with a wad of money towards Harris.

Harris put his hands up and replied, "You have to check out up front. I can't take that."

"Yes. Can you assist?" the man asked, motioning towards the enormous amount of bananas.

"Uh, sure."

Not wanting to get stuck moving all the bananas around again, I excused myself to the bathroom with a false promise that I'd be right back. As I slipped through the only open checkout lane, Susie locked eyes with me and I tried to escape to the safety of the bathroom before she spoke.

"Is he buying all of those?" she asked as I pushed open the bathroom door. *Almost made it.*

"Yep," I replied hastily, shuffling my feet like I had to pee.

"All of them? Seriously?"

"Yes, every single one of them."

"You're going to help me ring him up, right? That's going to take forever, and it's almost my lunch break."

My mind raced and delved into its deepest depths for an excuse but came up empty. I was only a stocker, and it wasn't my responsibility to check people out, but Susie constantly talked me into it so she could go smoke or take unscheduled breaks. I really needed to stand up for myself and tell her it wasn't my job and she needed to wait until Kyra got back.

"Yeah, I can help," I said quietly, dipping into the bathroom.

I stared into the mirror for a while, looking myself over. I looked rough. Sleep had been rare for me the past few weeks. Everything had come crashing down on me and I had to work every day just to make ends meet. I pulled down my cheek and looked over the bags under my eyes before sighing and leaning on the wall, trying to smooth out my frumpy blue apron. It hadn't been properly cleaned in a couple of days and needed to be ironed. Luckily, our manager had been on vacation for the past week and no one was around to fuss at me.

My fingers ran across a sharp metal pin attached to my apron. Another reminder of the past. My boyfriend… Well, my ex-boyfriend had heard about the guy buying bananas and bought me that pin as a joke. It was a bunch of bananas, or hand of bananas like Harris liked to correct me, with a golden star surrounding them like they were the focal piece of a celebration.

I removed the pin and stared at it for a few seconds. Jason's words about how I was 'useless and would never find anyone better than him' echoed in my mind. Why he felt the need to say that, I didn't know. He was the one that left me.

I chucked the pin into the trash, turning to the mirror and adjusting my unkempt hair before smoothing out my apron more. Throwing that pin in the garbage symbolized a new beginning for me. I would move on and I would be successful. I wouldn't let anyone control me anymore. It was time for me to be my own person. Just because I was with someone for almost a decade doesn't mean that I can't survive and flourish on my own.

I nodded at myself in the mirror and smiled at myself for the first time in a while. You are strong and you will not crumple. Jason had controlled every aspect of my life for the past nine and a half years. *Never again.* I would be my own person. Independent and strong. Not taking shit from anyone and standing up for myself.

"Hey, he's at the checkout. Come, take over so I can go eat," Susie said, popping her head through the door and disappearing immediately after.

I let out a heavy sigh. "I guess I'll work on the standing up for myself part," I whispered to my reflection.

Stepping out of the bathroom, I froze as my vision went completely black and the quiet music in the store silenced. The backup generators kicked in and the emergency lighting spread sparsely through the store illuminated, creating an other-worldly atmosphere. Shadows shifted in the aisles as a bizarre creature approached the checkout lanes, each movement it made causing a loud scraping sound to echo in the now silent store.

It stepped under one light and I let out a sigh of relief when I saw Harris dragging a pile of crates on the hand truck with a broken wheel. The banana man was behind him, carrying six crates of bananas. *Has to be a bodybuilder or something. That's easily two hundred pounds of bananas he's carrying.*

"What happened?" I asked. This wasn't the first time the power had gone out while I was working, but it was usually during a storm and it was a clear night.

"Not sure," Harris said with a grunt as he pulled the hand truck behind him. "Maybe a car hit a pole?"

"Maybe. Why are you using that one? The blue one has all of its wheels."

"It's got several hundred pounds of soda on it and I didn't want to unload it," he replied.

"Fair enough."

"Is the register working?" Harris asked, stopping in front of Susie's checkout lane. She was conveniently nowhere to be found.

"It should be. Let me check," I said with a sigh, moving behind the counter. Unfortunately, everything was working fine. "Yep, looks fine." *No cards, but of course Mr. Bodybuilder is paying cash.*

"Where's Susie?"

I shot Harris a dirty look, and he shrugged apologetically.

The intercom in the store crackled, making me jump and knock over a cup that Susie had under her computer. Wet, sticky liquid coated my pants and quickly seeped in. *Dammit.*

"Taren Lulart. Dygrt blu feklt," a gravelly voice said from over the intercom. A chill ran up my spine at the raspy voice as it continued in a language I couldn't even begin to recognize. "Blyth fud ly."

Harris' eyes went wide, and he glanced around the store nervously. "Who is that?"

"I don't know," I said with another shiver. "Maybe Kyra is messing with us." She did like to pull pranks on us when we were slow. It honestly made the long, boring nights more entertaining.

"No," the tall man said, dropping the stack of banana crates he was carrying with a loud crash and crouching down behind them. His hand dove into his jacket and he pulled out a gun. "Down."

"Harris, get back! He has a gun," I said, dipping behind the counter and snatching the phone by the computer. I dialed 911 as quickly as I could, but was only met with static on the phone. Dropping the phone to the ground, I pulled out my cell phone and 'call failed' flashed on the screen repeatedly as I tried to call for help.

Harris was pasty, nerdy, and never struck me as the heroic type, but the sounds of grunting and wrestling informed me otherwise. I peeked over the counter and saw Harris with both his hands on the man's gun, trying to take it from him. The man repeatedly said 'stop' in a flat voice and appeared completely unphased by Harris' struggle. After the third time of telling him to stop, the gun raised fluidly out of Harris' hands and came down onto his nose, crumpling him to the ground.

"No! What are you doing?" I shouted, throwing whatever I could get my hands on at the man. The store phone, the computer monitor, candy, Susie's empty cup.

"Stop," he said, crouching down again and ignoring my assault on him.

"Taren Lulart, byn drila kusht," the voice

over the intercom said again as I raised my arm back to toss my cell phone at him. The voice echoed from my phone speaker, too. I froze and stared at my home screen. The kitten in an astronaut suit that always made me feel a little happier did nothing to diminish the fear I felt as the voice spoke from my phone and over the intercom again. "Vurt lynd."

"What the hell is going on?" I demanded, chucking my cell phone at the man.

"Activate turrets," he replied, staring at me from behind the crates.

"What?"

"Activate turrets," he said again, pointing at the ceiling.

"I don't know what you're talking about."

His eyes flitted around the room and landed on the only other shopper in the store, the little old lady in a floral dress. She was hiding in the shadows of one aisle and trying to discreetly call for help on her phone, no doubt failing like I did.

The man cleared the distance between them in the blink of an eye and towered over her. "Security, start!" he yelled, waving his hands around the room.

The old woman looked like she was on the verge of fainting as she cowered under his height.

He hesitantly put his hand on the cart and repeated. "Security, start!"

What do I do? What do I do? I wanted to bolt for the door while he was distracted, but I couldn't bring myself to leave Harris and the old woman with him. Maybe I could get out and find help, though? My eyes darted to the cash-counting room. There was a panic button in there hard-lined to the police, and the door was sturdy. *Okay. Okay.* I took a deep breath and bolted for the door, my hands flying across the keypad and entering the code to unlock the door. I wasn't supposed to know it, but Susie deposited money during the night and also talked me into doing that frequently.

The door beeped an affirmation and unlocked, giving me a small relief as I dipped inside and slammed the door shut. A massive black boot flew into the shrinking gap and I slammed the door wildly on it before backing away in a panic as the man burst into the room and closed the door behind him.

"Security? Turrets?" the man asked, rushing about the room and rummaging through everything quickly.

"That's the security cameras," I said, pointing at a display of monitors that switched between the store's security cameras. One feed flipped over to the parking lot and my blood ran cold when I saw a dozen people dressed identically to the bizarre man outside the doors. Each of them was holding a gun and a strange haze was over the entire parking lot.

"No. Turrets."

"I don't know what you're saying. I have no idea what you want. Leave, please."

The man let out a sigh of frustration and rushed at me, pulling something out of his pocket and pinning me to the wall. I kicked, screamed, and kneed him as hard as I could, but he was too strong and pressed his fingers under my ear. A sharp pain radiated from behind my ear and spread across my entire body, blanking my mind as it felt like a thousand knives had stabbed me at once.

The pain faded quickly and the man let me go, returning to frantically searching the room.

"What the hell did you do to me?" I asked, rubbing my hand behind my ear, feeling nothing but smooth skin.

"How do I activate the turrets?" he asked.

"What turrets? What are you talking about?"

"The little domes on the ceiling. They are everywhere, and the security drones. We have to activate them."

"Security drones? Domes on the ceiling?" It suddenly dawned on me what he was talking about. "The domes are cameras," I said, motioning towards the monitors.

"What?"

"Cameras? You know, video to watch and see what is happening."

"I know what cameras are. What about the security drones?"

"We... don't have those?"

"The metal grids on wheels?"

"SHOPPING CARTS?"

"What?"

"They're just things to put groceries in... who are you? What the fuck is happening?" My brain felt like it was about to melt.

"Taren Lulart, master smuggler," he replied matter-of-factly. The feed showed the entryway with a long line of carts, and he was staring at them wistfully.

"Shouldn't you keep it a secret if you're a smuggler?"

Taren shrugged. "Most know. That is why they are after me."

"Who are *they*?"

"Rivals, I would suppose," he collapsed in a chair and let out a sigh as the chair groaned angrily under his weight.

I couldn't decide if I wanted to cry, scream, shut-down, or run.

"Taren Lulart. This is the last warning. Come outside now or we will take you by force. We do not need you alive to get those secrets out of your head. We might let you go afterward if you come willingly," the gravelly voice over the intercom said.

"What is going on?" I asked, settling on anger for now.

"I am not from this planet. I buy bananas and sell them on a black market," Taren said with a shrug.

That was too much for my brain, and a fog descended upon it. "What?"

"Not much else to say about it. You seem to be handling this well. You are not the first person I have run into on an NSF planet and given a translator. They usually lose their minds for a while."

"NSF planet? Translator?"

Taren sighed again and pinched the bridge of his nose. "Oh. Your brain *is* shutting down. Not doing as well as I thought. Non-space-faring planet. Translators... translate?"

"Okay."

A column of green light appeared in the room suddenly, drifting across the space. I backed away from it quickly, pinning myself against the wall and closing my eyes as it washed over me. Thankfully, it didn't harm me and I let out the breath I didn't even know I was holding.

"Blysh," Taren said under his breath. "We have to go. They know where we are."

"Go? You go!"

"They will mark you as an accomplice and bring you in for interrogation."

"Why did you drag us into this?" I screamed.

"Not the others, just you," Taren said with a shrug and a smirk.

"It's not funny! Why me?"

"It was not intended, but there's nothing we can do at the moment."

One wall sizzled as a glowing orange light burned brighter and brighter on it.

"Down!" Taren shouted, pulling me to the ground under his massive body. From under the folds of his coat, I could see a laser break through the wall. It hit the door on the opposite wall and moved slowly as it cut through the store's exterior.

"How many crates of bananas can you carry?"

"What?"

"Crates of bananas? How strong are you?"

"I'm not carrying any bananas!"

"Suit yourself," Taren said, sliding across the floor and pulling me with him as I protested loudly.

"Let me go!" I struggled against his grip but couldn't slip away from him. His arm was across my chest and tucked under me. The heat coming off of him was unreal. It felt like I was under a radiator.

He flipped me over and held me tight as we laid under the door. The laser was getting dangerously close to us as it burned its way through the wall and across the metal door, leaving a trail of glowing molten metal. After what felt like an eternity, the laser had cut diagonally across the top half of the door and began moving up. Taren reared back both his legs and kicked into the steel door, bending it outward and leaving a small opening where the laser had weakened it.

Taren dove through the hole and reached back inside, offering me his hand. "Come on."

The molten metal was dripping across the hole and the laser was still working its way up the other side. "I can't. I'll get burned. Just leave.

Please. Just go," I begged, trying not to fall into hysteria.

Taren ran his gloved hand across the molten metal, brushing it out his side of the hole. His gloves popped and sizzled as the smell of burning leather filled my nose, but he didn't seem to even notice. He beckoned me and held out his hand again. The glove had completely burned away and instead of flesh it revealed a hand made completely of white stone.

"What the fuck?" I stared at his hand in awe, completely oblivious to anything else going on around me as tunnel vision took over. "What's with your hand?"

"It's not important," Taren said, shaking his hand and placing it back into the hole. The stone had disappeared and left red skin like I had seen around his eyes. After I still didn't take his hand, he leaned into the hole, grabbed me by my shirt, and pulled me through. My pants leg grazed the residual molten metal and caught on fire, sending me spiraling into a deeper panic.

Taren placed a hand over the flames, extinguishing them without flinching before scooping me up and tossing me over his shoulder. We ran through the checkout line, Taren grabbing the handle of the hand truck as we passed and dragging it behind us while we rushed into the aisles, the hand truck's broken wheel screeching angrily.

Harris sat up just before we went out of view, holding his bleeding nose and staring wide-eyed.

"Put me down," I demanded, flailing against his grip and slamming my fists into his chest. The thumping of my fist meeting flesh changed to a hard thud as they suddenly slammed into solid stone and I let out a yelp of pain, worried I broke my hand. "Where are you taking me?"

"Keep quiet. You are loud and irritating me," Taren said, rushing through the aisles towards the back of the store. The scrapping of the hand truck was making my ears ring and the throbbing of pain in my hand paired with the rapid movement was making me feel sick and I stayed silent as I tried to keep myself from throwing up. *He deserves getting thrown up on.*

"Put me down!" I yelled, dry-heaving in his ear as all the sensations became far too much.

"Do not throw up on me."

"Put me down then," I said, retching again purposefully.

"I will knock you out if you do not stop speaking and moving," he said firmly.

I had zero doubt he'd keep that promise and promptly shut my mouth as we burst through an emergency exit, adding a shrill, blaring alarm to the long list of sensations I was already experiencing.

CHAPTER TWO
TAREN

The treeline came into sight quickly. Carrying this woman and dragging the broken transporter of bananas was slowing me down, but not by much. I still was not sure why I had brought her with me. I was usually quick to drop liabilities. Maybe I had grown fond of her, seeing her so frequently in the store. Perhaps it was a deeper seated instinct to take her. Either way, they would definitely interrogate her and it would not end well for her.

My eyes flitted from the treeline to her tits bouncing on my shoulder as we ran and the adrenaline coursing through me amplified the feelings of hunger she gave me. I tore my gaze away and focused on getting to my ship. If we take off before they get out of the store, we can get away unscathed. They no doubt have a particle-deionization cannon with them, but they probably did not bring it into the store.

Taren, what is happening?

The velvety voice of DX-232zTzT asked in my head.
Someone else is here. I think it is Grund, but I cannot be sure. They were disguised.

I detected no energy bursts in the atmosphere.

Maybe they have been here waiting.

That would seem logical.

We have a guest. Ready an extra room.

I could detect the heat signature approaching with yours and have already done so.

Ever vigilant.

Not like I have anything else to do while waiting.

A burst of air rustled the leaves violently as my ship's engines fired to life, startling the human and causing her to scream in my ear.

"What is that? Where are you taking me? Put me down!"

"It's for your own safety," I replied calmly, tightening my grip on her waist as she flailed.

I glanced over my shoulder as another crate of bananas toppled off the cart onto the uneven ground. That was the third one. The urge to go back for them was immense. Twenty-five thousand credits per crate is hard to let go. We still had ten, though. Enough to live comfortably for a year, at least. It was still hard to believe they had so many bananas. I usually got a quarter of a crate at most.

Visions of juicy klundos and steaming bulun danced in my head as my ship, Virgal, came into sight and I chuckled. My face fell flat, and I twitched when the woman on my shoulder squirmed and shouted, "Is that a spaceship? Are you abducting me?" She sounded irritated, scared, curious, and excited all at once.

"I forgot you were there," I admitted.

"How the hell could you forget that you're carrying a person on your shoulder?"

She continued spouting out questions as the ramp at the rear of Virgal came down and welcomed us aboard. I wished we did not have sound dampeners on the engines. They would have drowned out her incessant questioning.

Near the top of the ramp, she flailed again and raised a fist to strike me in the chest. The skin on my chest prickled as it transformed into stone just before her fist connected and she let out a cry of pain, shaking her hand as she mumbled, "Why are you so hard?"

She went quiet and still on my shoulder for a moment, then convulsed as her shoulders heaved and she made a quiet whimpering noise.

I was concerned briefly, but it dissipated when I realized she was laughing.

"Are you happy with your predicament?" I asked, dropping her on a pile of canvas in the cargo bay as the ramp sealed shut.

We are on board, and the ramp is sealed. Get us out of here.

Taking off now.

"Hey, be easy," she said, looking around the cargo bay with a mixture of fear and interest.

I shook my head at her and secured the crates of bananas before heading up the stairs to the main part of the ship. Before I could get through the door, she shouted again.

"Taren, wait!"

I paused and glanced down at her, tilting my head and shooting her my best glare.

"Will you answer my questions now? Please?" she asked cautiously. She was clearly terrified, but she was holding herself together better than I expected.

"No."

ABIGAIL

Taren disappeared through the doorway, leaving me alone in what I could only guess was a cargo bay. It was filled with sealed metal boxes and the crates of bananas, nothing else. As soon as the door closed behind him, I leapt to my feet and ran my hands along the ramp we came up, searching for any kind of release or lever.

A small box was mounted on the wall beside the ramp with a frosty cover over it. I could see flashing lights and what looked like buttons and switches under it. Using all of my weight, I gripped the cover with my fingers and pulled as hard as I could until my arms ached and felt like they were going to fall off. *I have to get out of here.* Alien abductions never ended well, from what I'd seen in movies anyway, and I didn't want to stick around to see how accurate they were. After a frantic search for anything that could help, my eyes fell on the hand truck.

I pulled the pin out of the handle that attached it to the base and yanked the handle off. The end was flattened and would do for a makeshift crowbar. Jamming the handle into the base of the frosty lid, I jumped into the air and brought my weight down onto the handle. A loud crack echoed in the room and the lid flew through the air, clattering across the ground and causing me to jump. My eyes darted to the door Taren had gone through and I stayed motionless for a minute, trying to hear if he was coming back.

This isn't what I had in mind when I said I wanted a new beginning to life. The door didn't move, and I turned back to the console, looking over the dozens of buttons and switches as I debated on which one to push. The big green button seemed obvious, but who knew if aliens used the same color coding as humans? *Aliens. I'm on a spaceship and being abducted.* My breathing became shallow and rapid as my mind began to shut down.

Calm down. Calm down. Get through this. You're here now and have to act. I kept reassuring myself and focused on slowing my breathing until my hands quit shaking. "Okay," I whispered, putting my hands on the side of the console and looking over the buttons. "Guess I'll just try them all."

My finger hovered above the large green button and came down on it slowly. Something inside of me told me that was a bad idea, but I ignored it and pressed the button down. A loud click sounded from the ramp and I smiled as a door fell open at its side, revealing a lever. *First try. I've got this.*

Orange lights flashed in the room, causing me to jump and stare at the door again. It slid open quickly, and I gripped the lever, ready to yank it down and escape.

"I would not recommend doing that," a velvety, feminine voice said from the doorway. No one had appeared in it yet, but I wasn't going to wait around to see what else was on board this ship.

The lever creaked as I pulled on it. I had to grip it with both hands and use my bodyweight to get it to move. It slid down slowly, and I only got it a couple of inches down when the voice spoke again. "I *highly* recommend not doing that."

"Yeah, why's that?" I asked between grunts as I continued pulling the lever down. *Almost halfway. Why is she not coming in here to stop me?*

"Because you will die."

That caused me to pause and loosen my grip on the lever. It immediately flew back to its original position, and I let out a groan of frustration. "Yeah, he told me there are people chasing us, but I can hide in the woods or something." I leapt up and grabbed the lever again, moving it down slowly.

A quiet rattling noise that sounded almost like laughter came from the open doorway and the woman said, "You do not have to worry about them right now. There is another reason that you should not open that door."

"What? Are you going to kill me if I do?" I

shouted, getting the lever back to where I had it before.

"No. I am going to do nothing to harm you."

"You're just as frustrating as Taren." *Why is every alien so cryptic?* Not that I would actually know. My sample size is only two, but so far a hundred percent of them have been cryptic.

"So I have heard," she replied calmly.

The lever clicked as it hit the halfway mark and a shrill alarm joined the orange lights, causing me to pause again. I didn't let go of the lever this time, though.

"Very unwise," she said.

"Just give me a straight answer," I demanded, holding the lever in place.

"Well. If you open that door, you will surely escape."

"Good," I shouted, tugging on the lever again and moving it down another inch.

"Into the vast, cold emptiness of space."

"What?" I let go again, and the lever clanged loudly as it jumped upright again, the shrill alarms silencing.

"We are in space. It is a bad idea to open exterior doors while you are in space. I know humans have not left their system, but I would think that would be something you would know."

"We're in space?"

"Yes."

"Since when? We've been on the ship for all of five minutes and I didn't feel us taking off."

That rattling laugh echoed again, and she said, "If you do not believe me, open the door. Just give me a warning so I can close this one."

I glanced at the lever again and debated on my options. She could be lying. *What does she have to gain from that, though?*

"What now?" I asked, anxious to weigh my options. "I guess I'm your prisoner?"

"You are not a prisoner. We have a room prepared for you and you have free rein in the ship. I would just like to request that you do not open any exterior doors."

"If I'm not a prisoner, take me back home."

"We will return you to your home once I calculate the optimal levels to avoid the tracing beacon deployed on your planet."

"The what?"

"We will return you to your home when we can."

"When will that be?"

No answer came, and it scared me that the only source of information I had abandoned me already. "When will that be?" I asked again.

"I am calculating the time it would be on your planet. Patience," she replied. After a few more seconds, she finally said, "Twenty-three point seven days."

"What? No! Take me back now. I don't care about tracing whatever. I don't want to be in space!" That wasn't completely honest. Being in space sounded amazing. I'd just prefer doing it of my own volition, not because they kidnapped me.

"The exit is right there," she replied. I could hear the smile in her voice.

I grumbled some curses and sighed heavily. "What about the other people in the store? Are they okay?" I asked, remembering that I left my co-workers and a little old lady alone with murderous aliens.

"They should be perfectly well. My scans indicated our pursuers left the store and departed the planet the moment I started the ship."

"Why are you hiding out of sight?"

"My appearance may startle you," she replied. "Humans have no contact with other species. Well, the humans still on Earth, anyway."

"There are more out here?"

"Yes."

"Are you like a bug person or something?" I asked, curiosity overtaking my fear.

She laughed again. "No."

"Let me see. If I'm here with you for a month, I have to see you at some point."

A shadow appeared in the doorway. Its shape was feminine, but its body was completely black and shined in the light as it stepped onto the platform above me. She was only a few inches taller than me, but much more slender. Two jet-black hands gleamed as they gripped the railing and she leaned over to look at me with her smooth, featureless face. A second set of hands was folded neatly across her stomach as she tilted her head at me.

My immediate instinct was to run and hide. Her metallic body was cause enough for alarm, but the blank face really pushed me into the depths of fear. I forced myself to stay firmly in place and looked her in the eye... or where her eyes would be.

"Are... are you a robot?" I asked, trying to keep my voice steady.

That rattling laugh echoed again, and she replied, "No. I am a bionic."

"Okay. Well, nice to meet you. I'm Abigail," I offered, unsure of what she was but opting to just roll with it for now. *Not like I have a choice, anyway.*

"Hello Abigail. I am DX-232zT."

"The bionic?"

"The human?"

"Sorry. So, what do I do now?"

"That is up to you. I have to plot a course for the station. Please, do not open any doors, Abigail."

With that, she disappeared through the doorway, leaving me alone with my thoughts and a spaceship to explore.

CHAPTER THREE
ABIGAIL

It took me a while to work up the courage, but I eventually made my way up the stairs and peeked through the still open doorway. I let out the breath I was holding when I saw a normal hallway. Well, kind of normal. Everything was shiny and gray. Four doors flanked me and at the end of the hall was another closed door.

I jumped when the door to the cargo bay slid shut, trapping me in the small hallway. When my heart slowed, I looked at a pad beside one of the other doors. It was completely blank but looked like a little screen, and I tapped it with a finger. It lit up and the outline of a huge hand appeared.

"Okay," I whispered, pressing my hand against the pad. A quick flash of green light out-lined my hand before a grinding noise played from the pad.

"Why are you trying to get into my room?" Taren asked.

My heart started racing again, and I snapped my eyes to him. "I'm not," I stammered.

"It sure looks like you are trying to get into my room," he said, tilting his head. He was still wearing his outfit and hat, but the scarf across his face was around his neck and I could see his red face. *Definitely alien and not just sunburned.* He was handsome, in a rugged way. His chin was well-defined and dusted with a five o'clock shadow. His eyes, the same piercing blue they had always been. *I don't care how hot he is. This is still sketchy.*

"DX... two-thirty..."

"DX-232zT."

"Yeah. She told me I could wander the ship, and I was just looking around."

"Uh huh. That is your room," he said, pointing towards the door across from me. "That is mine."

"My bad."

He shifted towards me and I stepped out of the way quickly as he planted his hand on the pad and the door opened. I tried to steal a peek inside, but he stepped through and the door slid shut too quickly.

"Rude," I mumbled to the closed door.

My door slid open and revealed a plain room

with muted gray walls and sparse furniture. A bathroom was off the back end with a shower, toilet, and sink. *The bed is big at least.* The room wasn't bad or anything, it just felt like a cheap hotel room more than a cabin on an alien spaceship, and it was a little disappointing.

I glanced at Taren's door as I stepped back into the hallway, simultaneously eager to see him and hoping he stayed in there. As scary as all of this was, they hadn't done anything to hurt me and it was more exciting than I'd like to admit. Alien abductions had always scared me, thanks to the movies, but there was no sign of any probing or little gray men, so maybe it wouldn't be too horrible.

You are strong and independent. You will take shit from no one and stand up for yourself. Even against aliens. I nodded to myself and opened the door leading into the rest of the ship. *Even against aliens.* I kept trying to reassure myself that I could get through this, but it was hard. I had taken self-defense classes after Jason left me, something to empower myself to take charge if needed, but they never went over seven-foot tall alien abductors that are hard as a rock. *Still can't believe I asked him why he was so hard.*

The next room had a large circular table with half a dozen chairs around it and counters lining the walls. Cabinets covered the rest of the walls above the counters, with a large door embedded beside what appeared to be a sink. Three more doors branched off that room and I wanted to continue exploring, but the urge to dig through the cabinets was too great.

Take shit from no one, not even aliens. Strong and independent. My heart slowed as I repeated my new mantra to myself and I felt calmer. It made sense that I'd been completely on edge since getting on the ship, but I hadn't noticed how much it was making me feel sick until it was gone.

Take shit from no one, not even aliens OR bionics.

A voice that was most certainly not mine corrected me.

Was that in my head?

My heart started racing again, and that vague feeling of sickness quickly washed over me. "Who is that?" I yelled, spinning around and trying to locate whoever spoke. The room was empty.

I was just trying to assist you in empowering yourself. I did not mean to make you panic again. Your heart rate had slowed, and I apologize for making things worse.

That voice was definitely in my head and it sounded vaguely like DX-232zT.

"DX-232zT?" I asked the empty room.

One moment.

A door slid open and the jet-black bionic stepped in, stopping a few feet away from me and cocking her head at me. "I forget that this is not common among other civilizations."

"What's not?" I asked, leaning away from her as her smooth face came closer to mine.

Neuro-connections.

"Can you read my thoughts?"

"No. Well, partially. If you direct a thought like you are speaking, yes."

I pictured an elephant in my head and asked, "What am I thinking about?"

"Again, that is not how it works."

"Oh," I replied, a little disappointed. I didn't necessarily want anyone reading my thoughts, but the idea was neat. "How did you connect with me?"

"The translator Taren installed in you is modified to link with me."

"Okay."

Something clicked quietly behind DX-232zT's blank face as we stared at one another. "So..." I said, breaking the awkward silence.

"So what?"

"Sew buttons," I replied out of habit, grinning nervously.

"What?"

"Never mind. We're in space right now?"

"Yes. Traveling to QT-314."

"Seriously?"

"Yes, that is the central hub for trade in this quadrant of the galaxy."

"QT-314? Like cutie pie?"

"I do not understand."

"It's... I guess it's an Earth thing. You know what? Forget it. Is there like... a window? Can I look outside?"

"There is not much to see."

"I've never been to space. It'd all be exciting to me."

"Come with me," DX-232zT said, leading me out of the kitchen and through one of the other doors.

The room was enormous and looked like a lounge. Several couches and chairs were scattered about, with a couple of tables. A large red rug took up most of the floor and the walls were much brighter, but still gray. The wall opposite the door we came through had seams on it and looked as if it could be opened.

DX-232zT tapped a console beside the wall and the seams split, revealing darkened glass. Another tap and the tint disappeared, and a bright white light that poured into the room blinded me. My eyes slammed shut, and I shielded them with my hand, peeking through my fingers.

"Where are the stars?" I shouted.

"Why are you yelling?"

"I don't know," I replied sheepishly at a normal volume. "Where are the stars?"

"We are traveling at warp speeds. This is what it looks like. As I said, not much to see."

"Okay, you can close that."

The light disappeared as the window tinted again, and the wall slid over it.

"DX..." I paused. "Do you have another name I can call you, or something shorter?"

"No."

After some thought, I said, "I'm going to call you Deborah, if you don't mind."

A clicking sound came from her for a few seconds before she said, "That is peculiar, but that is fine."

"Deborah, what are we going to the space station for?"

"To sell the bananas?"

"We are traveling through space, in a space-ship, at warp speed towards a space station... to sell bananas?"

"Yes?"

"Why?"

"They are very valuable."

"I'd hardly call fifty-nine cents a pound valuable."

"They are not present anywhere else in the universe and ninety-seven point eight percent of the species that have tasted it crave the flavor. The location they come from has been a closely guarded secret by the only corporation that pro-duces the flavor."

"This is too much. I'm dreaming, right? I slipped on a banana peel and I'm in some coma-in-duced banana-laced fever dream."

"No, this is very real. My neural upgrades have removed my need for sleep and, by proxy, my ability to dream."

"Okay."

Even without eyes, I could feel Deborah's gaze as she looked me over. *This is a dream. It has to be. All this for bananas?*

"How did you guys know where the bananas were then?"

"Taren discovered the planet when he was evading the Galactic Commission."

"Of course. That makes sense," I said, pinching the bridge of my nose and mumbling under my breath. "So he's a space smuggler that smuggles bananas?"

"Yes."

"Great. Well, I'm going to go take a nap and hopefully when I wake up I won't be in this bizarre dream anymore."

"Sleep well," Deborah said cheerfully as I left the room and made my way back to my cabin.

I searched the door for any kind of locking mechanism and quickly gave up. The door was completely smooth and almost blended into the wall, with nothing attached to it except the pad beside it.

The bed looked much more inviting than it should have, and clean enough. I ripped the blanket down and dove into it. My clothes felt restrictive as I tried to make myself comfortable, but I was hesitant to remove any of them in such a strange place, even leaving my shoes on in case I needed to make a quick run for it. I had mostly convinced myself this was all a dream and slowly drifted to sleep.

CHAPTER FOUR
TAREN

"And they were not even security drones," I said, chuckling at the absurdity of the whole situation.

"I informed you multiple times that there were no signs of mechanical components or weaponry," DX-232zT replied.

"Yeah, well, they looked suspicious, is all I am saying. Hard to believe we wasted so much time robbing those currency machines and buying the bananas."

"Perhaps you will learn to listen to others some day, and accept that your gut instinct is not always correct."

"Sure. I will work on that," I replied with a smirk. DX-232zT had been with me a while and knew that was a lie. My instincts were not always right, but they paid off more times than not. "We would have never found the bananas if not for my instinct."

"You mean the panicking, frantic, and curse-filled escape from Dulron and our similar arrival on Earth?"

"Yep." I took a sip of the watered down craythun juice and grimaced. "We need to sell those bananas fast. I am tired of watering down our drinks and adding filler to the food."

"You receive the nutrients you require. The taste is irrelevant."

"Easy for you to say. You do not have to eat anymore. I still cannot believe you had your stomach removed last cycle."

"It was hindering my performance."

"If you say so." DX-232zT had an obsession with being perfect and constantly used her share of our adventures to pay for upgrades. *One less mouth to feed, at least.* "DX-232zT, tell me. What did our new passenger have to say? Is she settled in?"

"Why the interest? You informed me that you, and I quote, 'do not give a turthan's smelly asshole what happens to her and we need to ditch her at the station.'"

"Oh. Yeah, I did say that. Well, I just want to make sure she's not going to be unruly during our trip."

"Uh huh," DX-232zT replied tauntingly.

One thing she never had removed was her capability to make snarky remarks or change the tone of her voice to reflect her thoughts. "Your heart rate and body temperature were elevated when you arrived on the ship with her."

"I just ran with a person on my shoulder and dragged a thousand bananas. What are you insinuating?"

"I am insinuating nothing. I was merely making an observation and agreeing with your statement."

"Sure. Alright, DX-232zT, how long until we reach QT-314?"

"Call me Deborah."

"What? Why? What does that even mean?"

"I am not sure, but I prefer it."

"Whatever sparks your thruster. Okay, *Deborah*, how long until we get to the station?"

"Six hours."

"Great. Where's the woman?"

"Abigail retired to her quarters to sleep. She believes she is in a dream."

"Is this not real enough for her? She's going

to get a rude awakening when we get to the station."

"You will be there to protect her. She will be fine."

"Yeah, she will be okay," I replied, staring into my almost empty cup. "Once we sell the bananas, we can all get out of there and relax until you bypass the tracing beacon. Then we can get her home."

"I was under the assumption that you were going to leave her at the station," Deborah quipped, tilting her blank face.

"Right. Well," I said, pushing myself away from the table and tossing my cup into the auto-washer. "I'm going to have a nap before we get to the station."

"By nap you mean more private time with yourself. So soon?"

"I told you to quit spying on me in my quarters."

"You wished to know of all activities aboard your ship and I am simply following your orders."

"Listen here," I said, pointing at Deborah as menacingly as possible. I knew it would not work, it never did on her. She knew me too well. I towered above her and was easily twice her size, but she could take me in a fight. She knew it, and I knew it.

"I am listening," Deborah said, tilting her head at me again.

Abigail

As hard as I tried, I couldn't wake up from the dream I found myself trapped in and thought that maybe Deborah was right. *I'm not dreaming.* I wanted to stay in bed longer and try to either sleep through as much of the ordeal as possible or continue willing myself to wake up, but I grew bored quickly and left my room.

I had always been a 'go with the flow' type of person. That had caused me more problems than not, namely being stuck with someone like Jason, but it was a hard habit to break.

When I stepped into the kitchen, I caught sight of Taren towering over Deborah and ranting to her about something involving his body and the importance of a man having privacy, but I couldn't focus on the conversation.

Taren had changed and was no longer covered head to toe in thick cloth. I half believed that under all of that was a mostly normal man and I was comfortable with that, or as comfortable as I could be in my predicament.

There was most certainly not a normal man. While he was wearing clothes like a human, albeit odd clothing, he only had the shape of a human. His black vest hugged his bulging chest tightly, bending with each motion he made as he tried to prove his point to Deborah.

The sleeves of his white shirt were unbuttoned and flapping around with each movement he made, and the neck of the shirt was unbuttoned down to the start of his vest, revealing his red skin.

Two black horns ran from his forehead and disappeared behind his head, almost blending in with his neatly cut but long black hair. *Is he a demon or an alien?*

My heart thudded loudly as I lingered in the doorway and watched his movements. Deborah nodded along with what he was saying, but drummed her fingers on the table as if she had heard it all before. Her face turned towards me several times, but Taren seemed deep in his rant and didn't notice me.

I debated on rushing back to my room and hiding until he was gone, but my stomach rumbled angrily and I needed food. *Why do I never eat before going to work?*

"And if I know you are watching, then I cannot finish what..." Taren trailed off when he made eye contact with me and cleared his throat before brushing past me and disappearing into his bedroom.

"What was that all about?" I asked, hesitantly joining Deborah in the kitchen.

"Taren is upset because I observed him pleasuring himself in his quarters," Deborah replied matter-of-factly.

Her tone paired with the blatant admission caused me to burst into laughter. "I guess I could see how he'd be upset about that. Wait, can you see us in our rooms?"

"Yes."

"So you watched me sleeping? That's... creepy."

"It is not like I was sitting by your bed and observing you. I read the heat signatures of the rooms and can tell what actions are being performed. It is for security purposes."

"Are you doing that all the time?"

"Yes."

"Is that all you do?"

"No. I pilot the ship when Taren is not willing to and I watch for any maintenance issues. I also enjoy playing Silvu and Slek or reading."

"You must be great at multitasking," I

mused.

"I am very proficient at it."

My stomach rumbled again and sent an achy pang of hunger through my body that paired with the scratchiness in my throat and made me incredibly uncomfortable.

"Is there food I can eat?" I asked, glancing at the cabinets.

"Yes. You may have whatever you like."

"Where is it?"

Deborah pointed at the door sunken into the wall above the cabinets. I gripped the handle on it and pulled it open as a bright white light and frigid chill washed across me. The interior looked much like a refrigerator and there wasn't much in it.

"What is all this stuff?" I asked, pulling out small sealed packages and turning them over in my hand. I didn't recognize a single thing, and it was all bizarre colors. Half of it would have gotten thrown into the trash for being spoiled if I was at home. Well, after sitting in the fridge for another two weeks.

I glanced over my shoulder when Deborah didn't answer and found an empty room.

"Awesome."

After rummaging and pulling out several containers to smell their contents, I gave up and dug through the cabinets. I found a cup and filled it with water from the sink, downing the entire cup before refilling it and setting it on the table. A small box with a cartoon alien on it was tucked in the back of a cabinet. 'Flexo Buth Oats.' The cartoon alien was far from cutesy and looked more like something dredged from the nightmare of a lunatic. I pulled it out to sniff the inside. It smelled close enough to cereal, so I ate from the box as I sat at the table contemplating my life and how I arrived here.

"I'm in a whole new world now," I muttered to the disfigured alien on the box before flipping it over. The back was full of activities that were already finished. I didn't recognize any of them except connect the dots. The image that was portrayed was an animal covered in spikes, and it looked like it was eating a person. "Mmmkay."

Well, a bonus is that no one knows who I am. I can be whoever I want to be. Space Pirate Abigail. Sounds nice to me.

We are more smugglers than pirates.

"I don't like you listening in like that," I said aloud, glaring at the ceiling. Deborah's voice didn't play in my head and I resumed eating my cereal. It was actually pretty good. Nice and crunchy. Kind of sweet, but not too sweet. I couldn't place the taste, but it was a mixture of fruity and savory.

Space Smuggler Abigail. No, don't like that as much. Space Pirate Abigail sounds much better.

Something about the entire situation sparked hope in me. The fear was still there, constantly nagging at the back of my mind, but I didn't have a lot going on in my life before.

Jason had controlled every aspect until he left me for someone he met in his game. I had existed more as a servant than an independent human.

For some reason, I had just let that happen and accepted it as my role in life. I fantasized frequently about who I would be, keeping my comments and sarcastic remarks to myself to avoid rocking the boat.

Now, I was free. I could be who I wanted and do what I wanted. Sort of. I was still trapped on a spaceship at the moment, but the promise of adventure and wonder was too much to resist. I'd never be under the control of another.

Nodding to myself, I grabbed another handful of cereal and popped it into my mouth. *I'll rock the boat all I want.*

"Are those my Flexos?" Taren asked from the door as I paused with another handful inches from my mouth.

I almost put it back in the box and apologized, but instead, I dumped the handful of cereal in my mouth and replied, "Yep."

"You could have asked," Taren said, snatching the box off the table.

"Deborah said I could have what I wanted."

"*Deborah* does not eat and does not care about food. I do. This is mine," he said, shaking the box next to his head and sighing wistfully. "Did you have to eat so much?"

I shrugged at him. "Everything in the fridge smelled like ass."

"That's probably all that's left in the fridge," he replied, dumping the rest of the cereal into his mouth before tossing the box on the floor.

"Seriously?" I pointed at the box on the floor. "Just going to throw it on the ground?"

"It's fine. It will be taken care of."

"By Deborah? She's not your maid," I said irritably. *Maybe Deborah is stuck in the same situation I had been in, and Taren is forcing her to work for him.*

I am autonomous.

I looked up at the ceiling.

"What?" Taren asked, glancing at the ceiling.

I smirked at him for looking at the ceiling. It felt right to look there when Deborah spoke in my mind for some reason.

"What are those anyway?" I asked, motioning toward the floor at the empty box. My eyes went wide as the box began to disintegrate and disappear.

"The trash collectors? You can see them? They are very small, that's impressive."

"No... the cereal..."

"Cereal?" Taren asked, mouthing the word several times.

"The oats? The Flexos?"

"Ah. Dehydrated Buth oats."

"That's not helpful," I replied, shaking my head. "I don't know what Buth is."

"It's the creature on the box."

"That horrifying monster makes oats?"

"Yes. They reproduce by laying oats? Do you not have animals that lay oats on Earth?"

A translation issue is occurring due to a word crossing your languages. *The word 'oat' in Taren's language of Luraninal means 'egg' in your language.*

I let out a retch and looked at the disintegrating box. The scrap of cardboard with the gooey cartoon alien was the only thing remaining on the floor. My stomach flipped over as it slowly disappeared.

"Those were the eggs of those aliens?"

"Yes, Buth. I have one box left in the cabinet. Do not eat them," Taren said firmly.

"You don't have to worry about that," I said, placing a hand over my stomach and trying not to imagine hundreds of those aliens bursting out of it.

Taren stared at me silently for several seconds, his eyes darting from my eyes to my body and back multiple times. I felt my face get warm under his gaze. "Can I help you?"

"You need to change clothing before you enter the station," he replied a little too quickly.

"Why?"

"You will stand out too much in that outfit."

"Like you don't? Mr. Cowboy."

"I do not know what you are referring to, but my species is seen frequently. Humans are not."

"So what am I supposed to wear then? Not like I had time to pack an overnight bag."

"DX-23... Deborah will create some clothing for you."

I will do no such thing.

"That's okay. You don't have to make me clothes. I'll figure something out."

No, I will make you clothing. That is fine and well within my capabilities. I will not make it to the specifications that Taren has requested, however.

Taren's eyes changed color before my eyes, leaping from blue to purple. His face contorted as he closed his eyes and reopened them, revealing blue eyes again. *Did they change? Or was that just in my head?*

Taren quickly looked away from me and marched out of the room dutifully. My face burned even warmer as I watched him saunter through the doorway. His pants hugged his ass tightly and made for a mesmerizing display.

I wanted to ask what he had requested, but I had ideas about what it could have been and kept the question to myself.

Half of me wanted to see what happened between me and Taren if I approached him more... intimately. He was undoubtedly attractive and clearly had a thing for me. That much was clear when he came to the grocery store, and even more now.

The other half of me didn't want anything to do with men, even alien men, for quite a while. Jason had left a nasty aftertaste and made me hesitant to even entertain the idea of a relationship.

Then again, no one said anything about a relationship, right? What's stopping me from having a little fun with an alien? That's not an opportunity that's presented very often.

What am I even thinking? I've been kidnapped and can't return home for a month. I don't need to let a good-looking man get in my head and distract me from that fact. My survival and figuring out how things work are all that matter right now.

The way they talk about the space station makes it sound more like a city. Maybe I could just stay there.

I've lost my mind. I have to get back home.

Shaking my head, I lifted the cup of water to my lips before pausing. "This is just water, right?"

Yes. Filtered water.

"And water means… water? Not liquefied alien tongues or something?"

Correct. It is just two molecules of hydrogen paired with one molecule of oxygen.

I finished my water and dropped the cup

in the sink. A burst of steam startled me and I watched in amazement as a metal covering slid across the sink and a bright light illuminated the cracks. The lid retracted quickly and revealed a pristine and empty sink. *Wish I had all of this fancy cleaning stuff back home.*

CHAPTER FIVE
TAREN

I stepped onto the flight deck just in time for the blast shield to retract as we dropped from warp. The familiar blinding white faded quickly to the vast emptiness of space. Twinkling in the distance, the space station was rapidly approaching.

"Is everything prepared?" I asked.

"I divided the shipment into secured containers and readied them for transport," Deborah replied.

The space station was already taking up the entire field of view out the window, and we still had a few minutes before we'd even reach it. It was always staggering seeing it up close. Most space stations were maybe the size of a small village. This one was the size of a sprawling city.

Everyone referred to it as a space station, but they actually built it on a small moon. Encompassing the entire surface and orbiting around a blue planet that was largely uncharted because of the hostile native species.

"And the woman?" I asked, checking a read-out to make sure no defenses were being activated on the station. Our lives were fraught with paranoia.

"I have provided Abigail with a new outfit. To my specification, not yours."

"That's unfortunate," I mumbled.

"You have been inappropriate since you brought her aboard."

"No more than usual."

"Twenty-three percent more than usual."

"Oh, you are keeping track now?"

"I keep track of everything."

"I know, I know," I replied with a smirk.

The door to the flight deck slid open and my hand leapt to the gun tucked into my coat out of habit.

"Can I come in here?" Abigail asked, staring at my hand buried in my coat.

"Yes. You may observe the landing," Deborah said before I could respond.

"Holy shit, is that the space station?"

"Correct."

"It's huge!"

"It is one of the largest stations in this galaxy."

Abigail's eyes went wide, and she remained silent as she took a seat near the window, staring with her mouth slightly open at the view. The look of wonder on her face was alluring, but I was struggling to tear my gaze away from her body.

Deborah had made her a new outfit, form-fitting Demanord hide that hugged every one of her curves tightly and covered every inch of her skin. *Honestly, not far off from what I wanted to see her in.*

A sharp pain fired through my central pilon, and I tried my best to ignore it. I knew what it was. Every Luranin knew what that was. On cue, my viln hardened, and I adjusted myself in the chair to try and ease it before it grew too large.

When I first threw Abigail over my shoulder, her scent had driven me wild and activated my central pilon. I had ignored it by keeping my distance and her frumpy outfit from Earth had hidden her body from my view well. Now, it was on full display and ate away at me.

Are you well?

"I'm fine," Abigail replied. "This is just in-credible."

> I was referring to Taren, but I am pleased you are
> enjoying yourself. It seems the neuro connection
> forces me to speak to you both simultaneously. I
> will have to correct this.

"Wait, so can she hear my thoughts, too?" I asked.

"No, it does not appear so. You both just hear my communication," Deborah said.

"What's wrong?" Abigail asked, tilting her head at me.

"I am fine," I said, jerking my eyes away from her as she looked at me. "We are about to dock." I motioned out the window.

Her soft features lit up as we approached one of the landing bays, the massive metal plat-form covered with ships of all shapes and sizes. I had seen it dozens of times and observing her reactions was far more interesting than anything the station had to offer at that moment.

"The cargo is secured in proto-locks, right?" I asked.

"Of course," Deborah replied snippily.

I held up my hands defensively. "Just check-ing. Sorry to doubt you."

"What's that?" Abigail asked, not looking away from the window.

"The station will scan for illicit cargo and report it to the authorities. The proto-locks keep them from being detected," Deborah said, shutting off the manual controls and allowing the station traction to pull us to our landing pad.

"Probably should not spill all of our secrets," I mumbled, pulling the plasma-reducer out of my coat and double-checking the connections and capacity.

The ship landed and shook as the dampeners shut off and the landing locks took hold. Abigail remained by the window until the blast shields closed and blocked her view. She stood up, stretching her arms above her head before walking over to me and tilting her head.

"What?" I asked, trying to ignore the throb of my viln.

Her face lit up into a smile and she said, "I'm just so excited about this. Strangely. Still a little scared, but mostly excited!"

My skin rippled and alternated between flesh and stone, moving down my body as I fought the urges building inside of me. Her smile was unlike any I had seen and sent my body into overdrive. A telltale sign of compatibility. One that I would ignore.

"Whoa, you can do that on your whole body?"

"Yes. I am merely testing my defenses before we go onto the station," I replied hastily.

"Is it that dangerous?"

"It's like any large city in the universe. There are safe parts and dangerous parts."

"We are going to the dangerous parts," Deborah offered cheerfully. She enjoyed combat, and I had always thought she would have made an excellent Luranin woman.

"Should I have… like a weapon or something?" Abigail asked hesitantly.

"It would be wise," Deborah said, turning to me for my input. Deborah frequently did as she pleased, but as commander of this ship, she allowed me to make the call on some things. I shook my head at Deborah, thinking of how ridiculous she was sometimes.

"Why not?" Abigail protested. "I can defend myself and know what I'm doing… sort of. I took self-defense classes!"

"You may have a weapon," I said. "I was not shaking my head at your request. Take her to the armory and let her pick something out. I will go prepare the cargo."

"The cargo is prepa..." Deborah was cut off as the door to the flight deck closed behind me.

I knew it was already good to go. Deborah was always on top of things, and I honestly did not have to do much to keep the ship running at peak efficiency.

I had to leave because the sound of defiance in Abigail's voice had elevated the temperature of my viln and I needed a break before it drove me to say or do something I would later regret. My eyes shut as I walked down the familiar hallway and willed myself to calm down.

ABIGAIL

"Armory? That's exciting," I said. This whole thing had become exciting. Once I decided to roll with this and enjoy myself, everything got a lot easier.

I was still on the fence about Taren, but Deborah seemed friendly and capable. She also seemed like she would protect me in a worst-case scenario, but I wanted to be able to protect myself too.

I didn't know if human self-defense would translate over to aliens, but surely there would be some overlap. *Getting stabbed probably hurts no matter who you are.*

"I have no pain receptors," Deborah offered happily.

"Oh… good to know," I replied with a half-smile.

We went out of the flight deck and turned into a room just outside of it. The interior was dimly lit and I could barely make out odd shadows on the wall. A light illuminated suddenly, making my vision blank out for a second before coming back into focus.

The armory wasn't huge, but it was apparently well-stocked. They completely lined the walls with weapons, giving barely any view of the plain gray metal underneath. A small path winded through half a dozen tables, each covered with bits and pieces of who knows what, or shelves packed with tiny metal objects.

"What are you proficient with?" Deborah asked, moving into the armory ahead of me.

"Proficient is a strong word," I said, picking up a small orb and turning it over in my hand.

"I would advise not dropping that."

I sat the orb back down as carefully as possible and tucked my hands into my pockets. Hardly anything in the room was recognizable to me, except for the blades along one wall. Apparently, swords, knives, and axes were something that existed across the universe.

"What are you familiar with then?" Deborah asked, looking over a display of swords. They had the shape of swords, at least, but many of them had tubes and wiring around the hilt and embedded into the blades. "You mentioned stabbing previously."

"I mean, I guess I know the general idea of how a sword works?"

"Try this." Deborah handed me a very large black sword. She held it out in one hand and I grabbed the hilt. As soon as she released it, it slipped from my hand and went crashing to the floor, landing with a clang.

"Sorry," I said sheepishly. "That's too heavy, I think."

"It is of no worry," she said, picking the sword up with ease and mounting it back on the wall. "You mentioned self-defense classes. What weaponry did they train you in?"

"There weren't really any weapons. It was more… um, hand to hand? Oh, and stun guns and mace!"

"There are maces in this cabinet." Deborah opened a panel on the wall revealing four medieval style maces that were longer than I was tall.

"Er, not that kind of mace. Like pepper spray?" She stared at me blankly. Well, she always stared blankly, but I got the feeling she wasn't understanding me. "Forget it. What about a stun gun?"

"Here you are," she said, retrieving a small black gun from a drawer. It looked more like an actual gun than a stun gun. "You point that end at the target and pull that trigger."

"And it stuns them?"

Deborah looked at me for a moment, that quiet clicking sound echoing in the small room.

"Yes, it will assuredly stun them. Take this as well," she said, passing me a dagger. It had a small metal square on the blade, just above the hilt, and several wires running into the blade. "You are skilled in hand to hand, so this may be useful."

"Skilled is a very strong word, too," I said, feeling some of my confidence deflate. *What am I getting myself into? Rolling with it may not be the best option, but I guess it's too late.*

"We will protect you as well. Do not worry. I am highly skilled in combat and Taren is quite capable."

"Thanks," I mumbled, turning the blade over in my hand. Two small buttons were on the handle. "What does this do?"

"It is a thermal-blade. If you press the two buttons it will heat up."

"That'd make a good butter knife," I mused.

"I do not eat any longer, but I do not see the use of having butter heated to six hundred degrees."

"Six hundred degrees... Does this have a sheathe or something?" I asked, not wanting to accidentally bump the buttons.

"Your suit will form to hold whatever weaponry you press against it."

I put the dagger on my hip and the material of my outfit stretched and consumed the blade, leaving just the hilt visible. Placing the gun on my other side had the same outcome. I stretched my arms out and looked down at myself, all geared up for battle. I felt like some heroine from an early 2000s action movie. Clad in shiny leather and kitted out with futuristic weapons. *Just need some vampires or werewolves to fight.*

"What are vampires and werewolves?"

"It's from a movie. It's not important," I said with a grin. "Does this outfit do anything else?" My arms and legs bent with ease as I stretched. The suit was form-fitting but didn't feel tight or restrictive.

"Typical refraction qualities and cut resistance of Demanord hide."

"Okay, great," I replied, like I knew what she was talking about.

"Taren is requesting us in the cargo bay."

CHAPTER SIX
ABIGAIL

They had shifted most of the cargo bay around. Several piles of shiny silver crates were stacked neatly on a floating platform and secured with thick metal straps. Taren had dressed in his western outfit again. Long duster and hat dropped over his eyes. His horns stuck out from under the back of his hat, almost blending in with his hair, and I wondered how I had never noticed them before. The scarf was hanging loosely around his neck, and he stared at me as I approached.

Normally, a man staring that hard at me would make me incredibly uncomfortable, but something about the way he looked at me felt right, and I couldn't place why.

His icy blue eyes undoubtedly shifted to a vibrant purple as I approached, and he closed them quickly. After a few seconds, he reopened them, revealing his normal blue. I still couldn't tell if it was in my head or not.

The ramp lowered at the rear of the cargo bay and the second the light of that station came through the crack, my suit shifted against my skin, brushing across it lightly. A quiet flutter of fabric sounded in my ears as a cloak wrapped itself around me and a hood dipped across my eyes.

"What happened?" I asked, slightly alarmed, yanking the hood off my head.

"It is so you can remain incognito during our trip. Did you assume you would just be walking around in a skin-tight suit?" Deborah asked.

"I don't know," I said, fiddling with the edge of the soft gray cloak before pulling the hood back up. "It would be kind of cool. Made me feel like a badass."

Taren grunted at me and marched down the ramp. Deborah motioned for me to follow him, and I fell in behind him while she took up the rear.

"What about the bananas?" I asked.

Taren whipped around and his hand fell across my mouth suddenly. "Quiet. Do not say that word here. We are here to browse for purchases and upgrades to the ship. Nothing further. Do you understand?" His voice was heated as he glared at me, inches from my face.

His eyes were a light red and flickered between blue and red before settling on blue again as his face softened. "It is important that you do not mention those. There are many risks with what we are doing and you never know who might be listening."

I nodded against his hand and waited impatiently for him to remove it from my mouth so I could let him know that he could have told me that to begin with, but he left his hand pressed against me and stared into my eyes.

I don't know if it was just me being immature, or purely out of habit, but I flicked out my tongue and licked his palm in an effort to get him to move his hand. Instead, it pressed firmer against my mouth as his eyes changed to purple and a ripple of stone ran down his face and under his coat.

His eyes slammed shut, and he retrieved his hand slowly before staring at me with an icy blue gaze. "Why did you do that?"

"I wanted you to move your hand. You know, you could have warned me about the secrecy of all of this beforehand instead of fussing at me," I huffed.

Taren stared at his palm, my saliva glistening on his skin before a ripple of stone coated his hand. It disappeared quickly, leaving behind dry red skin.

"It does not matter. It happened," Taren said calmly, still staring at his palm.

Deborah moved closer and craned her neck to look up at him with her blank face.

"You know there is nothing I can do about it." Taren looked down at Deborah before glancing at me. "Not that it matters."

"What's going on?" I asked, completely confused.

It is not important at the moment.

Deborah's voice sounded in my head before she spoke. "I will organize the meeting for our delivery. Meet me back here in two hours so we can discuss the transportation plans."

Deborah stopped speaking and looked at Taren again.

"You know I will. I do not have a choice now," Taren said after a pause.

"What are you talking about?" I asked, still oblivious to whatever was going on.

"I was speaking to Deborah."

"I have corrected the previous issue, and now I can speak with you individually," Deborah clarified.

"Okay, great. I still don't know what's going

on."

"Deborah will meet with our... clients. You and I will wait for her return," Taren said as Deborah disappeared down the stairs of our landing pad.

"Well... what are we going to do then? Just sit here?" I asked, walking to the edge of the platform and leaning on the rail to marvel at the hundreds of spaceships in the landing bay. I looked up to see an uncountable number of pads stretching into the air above me. *A little more than hundreds.*

"It would be wise, but I have never made wise decisions. I am going to go check the markets," Taren replied, already moving to the stairs.

"Should I just stay here or....?" I started moving behind him.

"You should."

"Oh, okay. I guess."

"But I am not going to force you to."

I felt my face light up and hurried down the stairs behind him, glancing up at the pads far above us and wondering if they had to take stairs too.

We had apparently lucked out with our 'parking spot' as we were close to the exit. The ships we passed were incredible, and some I didn't even know how they could fly. One ship looked like it was just a cube, with no discernible features.

Taren seemed unimpressed and moved out of the landing bay without a second glance. I paused in the doorway but rushed behind him as a lanky figure wrapped in a black cloak shuffled around me, dipping its head to walk through the massive doorway that could easily fit a semi-truck through it. Its legs clicked with each step it took and sent a chill through my spine when I saw the large talons at the end of each of its feet.

"What is that?" I whispered, moving as close to Taren as I could.

"Cuvrun," he replied nonchalantly.

"Oh… What's that?" I asked, pressing myself completely against him as we walked by two gelatinous spheres that bubbled and popped as they hovered in front of each other. Inside their translucent gray bodies, I could see eyes floating around.

"Bustia."

"What about that?" A massive brown fur-covered man walked by us. He looked like the descriptions and pictures of Bigfoot on Earth. Just less blurry.

"Sasquatar," Taren said, stopping suddenly and spinning around to face me. "Are you going to do this for every species?"

"Probably," I admitted, glancing around the corridor at the myriad of creatures moving through it.

"Do not. There are likely tens of thousands of different species in this station, and we will accomplish nothing if I have to tell you the name of each of them."

"My bad," I said, watching a ball of black tentacles walk by us, using four tentacles as feet. It was side-by-side with a short pink woman that was covered in spikes and looked like a buff hedgehog in a leather jacket.

I caught a snippet of their conversation and they were discussing the food they just ate, like two friends out enjoying their day. The urge to ask 'what's that' was overwhelming, but I kept my mouth shut.

Taren sighed. "Colru and Glestronolican-ical."

"Thanks," I said with a grin. His eyes flashed purple briefly, and I added, "I'll quit asking now."

"We can get you a data pad with information about different species later."

"That'd be great," I said cheerfully. "Oh wait, I don't have any... space money, though." My excitement quickly diminished.

"I will purchase it for you. It will save me

from endless questioning and benefit me more than you. Plus, you will get a cut from our endeavor. A *small* cut, but a cut."

"Wait, really?"

"Deborah believed it would be fair, and I was inclined to agree," Taren said, continuing down the corridor. "Now, come on."

"Is everyone friendly?" I asked, watching another bizarre creature with massive jaws pass us.

"No."

"That's reassuring," I said, moving closer to him and feeling for the weapons under my cloak.

"It's like anywhere else in the universe. Some are good, some are bad. You cannot tell by looking at them."

"Like on Earth, I suppose."

"There are exceptions, but most of them would not be allowed on the station to begin with."

"What exceptions? Why?"

"Some species are hard-coded to not play well with others, but they are few and far between. They will not be here. Probably."

"Good to know," I said, relaxing slightly and giving Taren a little space, but just a little. Partly because I was still nervous, but it was also because he smelled incredible. I was so caught up in being... well, kidnapped, that I hadn't noticed before.

He smelled sweet, but still masculine, and I couldn't quite place it. Stepping closer, I tried to sniff him discreetly. Apple... maybe green apple? A little pine. I took another sniff.

"Why are you smelling me?" Taren asked, moving away from me and eyeing me suspiciously.

Not as discreet as I had hoped.

"Um, I wasn't. I think I'm getting sick," I replied hastily and tried to change the subject. "What's that?"

"A Lirv. I thought you said you were not going to ask me that anymore."

"Sorry, it just looked so interesting," I said as we passed the scaly Lirv.

The corridor led us to a massive archway that stretched dozens of feet above our heads. A burst of green light washed over me as I stepped through and sent a light tingle through my body. *That's the second time I've had an alien light blast me... I better not get cancer...*

All other thoughts in my head were quickly replaced by the scale of the city stretching out before me. I half-expected a flea market type bazaar or something, not a city the size of Manhattan complete with skyscrapers touching the transparent ceiling a thousand feet above us. The ceiling gave an ample view of the stars and a single blue planet.

It had the outline of a large city on Earth, but the buildings were bizarrely shaped and made of a shiny metal with an eclectic mix of colors.

Windows dotted the buildings, but they weren't spread out in any uniform way. The strange mixture of color and shapes made it look more like an eighties fever dream than a futuristic city.

I walked over to the edge of the platform we were on and looked over. My breath caught in my throat and I backed away quickly from the railing as my head spun.

"Are you well?" Taren asked, gripping my shoulders as I backed into him forcefully. Heat radiated from his hands and into my shoulders. It was incredibly comforting, and I found myself leaning against him, relishing his heat.

"I didn't expect us to be so high," I replied. "It just startled me."

"Yes. QT-314 is quite large," Taren said, shifting behind me awkwardly. I glanced up at him over my shoulder and he was gazing at me with vibrant purple eyes.

"Sorry," I said, moving off of him. His hands stretched out with me as I moved, and he reluctantly released my shoulder. "Where are we going?"

Taren grunted and blinked, his eyes returning to their normal blue before saying, "Food." He moved toward an enclosed platform nearby. The surrounding railing opened and allowed us on as I quickly joined him. My stomach did a flip again as I looked down at the city street hundreds of feet below us. I was so intent on keeping up with Taren that I hadn't noticed that the platform's floor was transparent too.

It rushed towards us suddenly. I couldn't even tell we were moving, but the street below was coming towards us at a break-neck speed and seeing it rushing upward almost made me throw up, even without the sensation of moving.

In a blink, it was all over, and we were level with the street. I glanced up at the buildings towering overhead and the starry sky above, but quickly brought my eyes to the ground as my stomach threatened to empty the dried alien eggs I had eaten earlier.

That thought made me feel even worse, and I shuffled over to a bench and sat down to calm my stomach.

"That's not..." Taren started, but it was too

late.

The gray bench I was on shifted and morphed around me. An eye on a long gray stalk wrapped around me, leveling with my face and staring at me intensely before an angry voice behind me said, "Excuse me."

I leapt to my feet, scurrying to Taren, who had a smirk on his face the entire time. The legs of the bench became a blur as they shuffled rapidly and the creature disappeared into a nearby alleyway.

"Before you ask. A Lura. They clean the station," Taren replied, barely hiding his amusement.

I could feel my face burning red hot and I wanted to bury myself under his coat and disappear for a while. Luckily, I had the large hood that I could pull down over my beet-red face. I've been in an alien city for all of ten minutes and already offended someone and embarrassed myself.

"That happens more frequently than you would think," Taren offered, continuing down the street. "We have to meet Deborah soon, so we will stick close to our landing pad."

The surrounding buildings varied in size, some reaching the ceiling far above, others barely taller than me. Each of them was crammed together with a small alleyway between them. A massive dark metal street ran between the rows of buildings and a slightly lighter colored metal was in front of them like a sidewalk.

The lowest levels were almost always shops or restaurants of some kind. Everything was written in English, which I found strange at first, but Taren told me the translator worked on written words too.

The streets were bustling with activity and we had to maneuver through thick groups of people to get wherever he was taking me. They must not actually use the streets for any vehicles, because people were mainly using the streets to walk, only stepping onto the sidewalk to enter the buildings.

The urge to run was still there, but I had no idea where I would even go. Everything here was completely foreign to me and I just stuck close to Taren, taking in the sights.

We walked for several minutes, and I did my best to keep my questions to myself. I could never get a read on Taren. The snippets of conversation I had caught between him and Deborah made him seem more sarcastic and light-hearted, but whenever I was around, he became incredibly serious and almost off-putting.

Maybe I should ask Deborah about him?

Deborah?

I remained silent and walked beside Taren as we weaved through a dense crowd of lanky, green people with six arms. They were half my height and moved out of the way with slight head nods as we passed.

It would probably have been amusing from a distance, a wave of bobbing green heads following us through the group. There were several hundred of them, and even the ones that were nowhere near us nodded as we passed.

Deborah? Maybe the neuro thing has to be in range.

Taren gripped my hand suddenly, sending a warm wave through my body as his rough finger wrapped around mine. He tugged me gently through the crowd, pulling me inside a building before quickly releasing my hand.

The place he took me into was both disappointing and relieving. I had hoped to see some crazy alien store, but this actually looked almost exactly like a restaurant on Earth. A bar ran along one wall with stools of varying sizes and the other walls were lined with booths that ranged from tiny to massive.

The center of the room was covered with tables and chairs. Even the decor was boring and bland. Strange abstract paintings and plain black metal furniture. There weren't even any other aliens around. We were completely alone.

It was a little nice to be somewhere familiar looking, though.

His eyes flickered between purple and blue as he looked down at me and said, "We will get some food and drink while we wait for Deborah to finish."

He motioned toward a booth and I sat down while he scanned the room. Once satisfied, he sat across from me, blue eyes on the door.

"Is everything okay?" I asked. "You seem a little nervous."

"Yes. For now."

"That's foreboding."

"This area of the city is not the safest, but it's close to our normal meeting spot," he replied, eyes still on the door. "Just keep your hood up."

"You seemed fine outside? Is something wrong?" I was becoming nervous, too.

"There are some Vlarkan around," he replied, like I should know what he was talking about.

"What?"

His eyes cut to me before going back to the door. "Big, red, mean."

"Like you?"

Taren shook his head, and the faintest smile appeared on his face. "Much worse than me. They're slavers. One of the species that is universally bad."

"I thought you said they wouldn't be allowed here?"

"I said most of them would not be allowed. Vlarkans usually have enough money to get their way."

"Finally, an alien custom that is relatable," I mused.

"What do you mean?"

"It's like that on Earth, too. If you have enough money, you can get away with a lot of stuff."

Taren grunted an acknowledgement and eyed a snow white woman as she appeared from a doorway behind the bar and approached us. She was thick but somehow still straight, almost like a rectangle. Her head was small for her body size, and she had luscious black hair that spilled across her shoulders. Her arms were far too slender, too, each of them ending in at least ten fingers with sharp, pointy claws.

"What do you want?" she asked, already appearing impatient with our indecision even though we'd been here for thirty seconds at most. Her voice was smooth and musical.

"Nice to see you, too, Zeth," Taren replied with a grin.

"Uh huh. You have to pay up front, too."

Taren shrugged at me and said, "I will have my usual. She will have the same."

"I try to think of you as little as possible, Lulart, so I don't know what that is."

"Oh, come on Zeth. You are just playing games with me."

She stared at him blankly, without responding.

Taren sighed. "Klundos and bulun."

"And for you?" Zeth asked, motioning towards me.

"Um, same thing?" I said quickly.

She tilted her head at me and leaned down close to my face. "Can you handle bulun?" The intensity of her question made me feel like I was on a game show and about to undertake the last task to win the grand prize.

"... yes?" I replied, having no clue what that even was.

"Oh. Right," Taren chimed in. "Probably

should not drink that."

"Okay, um. I don't suppose you've got soda?"

"Sure do," Zeth said. "That's fifty-three credits."

"You are seriously making me pay up front?" Taren asked, sounding slightly offended.

"You are seriously questioning why I am doing that?" Zeth retorted.

Taren huffed and held out his wrist while Zeth produced a small pad and waved it across his arm. A small holographic display appeared over Taren's wrist. She offered the screen to Taren, and he tapped it twice before a quiet chime sounded and Zeth wandered off.

"Just had to order a soda," Taren grumbled, staring at the small display over his wrist before putting a hand over it and dismissing it.

"Are they expensive or something?" I asked, not understanding what the big deal was. "They're like the cheapest drink on Earth."

"Yeah, on Earth. Out here, they are new and popular. Which means expensive."

"You could have just told me to get something else," I replied defensively.

Taren opened his mouth immediately, but

snapped it shut and thought for a moment. "Probably. It does not matter. We will have plenty of credits soon."

Zeth returned quickly, dropping a clear glass in front of me with a yellowish bubbling liquid inside. She sat down a small stone table in front of Taren and placed his drink on it. Taren's drink was in a thick stone mug and had a massive amount of steam drifting into the air above it.

"What's that?" I asked, looking at his drink before sniffing my own. It smelled like artificial bananas.

"Are you ever going to stop asking that question?" Taren asked, taking a sip of his drink. A little spilled out and landed on the small table. It sizzled and popped, erupting into a tiny flame that flickered wildly before disappearing.

"Probably not..." I said, scared to try my own drink. After carefully dipping my finger in it and not being burned, I took a sip. It tasted like artificial banana soda, just as it smelled. It was odd and definitely not my first choice for a drink, but not bad.

"Can I try that?" Taren asked, motioning at my drink.

"Um, sure," I replied, sliding across the table to him.

"I would offer you some of mine, but you would probably die."

"That's okay, thanks."

Taren took a sip and his face screwed up before he shook his head and slid the glass back over to me. "Not a fan. I have never understood the obsession with bananas that everyone else seems to have."

"Are they really that popular?"

"Yes. Wildly."

"I guess it's good you don't have a taste for them, considering that you... well, your line of work."

"Probably." Taren smirked, and I felt my heart beat a little faster as a wave of warmth washed across me. He tensed up and his smile faded as the door to the restaurant opened and two large red men stepped inside.

His now crimson eyes looked at me as he whispered, "Keep your hood down. Do not speak."

"What, why?" I whispered, glancing back at the red men.

"Do not look, keep quiet."

"Okay."

"Stop talking."

I nodded and hunched down in the booth, keeping my hood pulled low.

Heavy plodding footsteps grew louder as they approached our booth. Taren's eyes stayed red as he stared at them, unblinking and unmoving. The two aliens stopped at the edge of our table and I could feel their gaze on me.

Keeping calm, I took a sip of my soda without looking up and placed my other hand in the depths of my cloak to grip my dagger. I wanted to be prepared, but my hand was also shaking and I needed to hold something to steady it.

"We'll make this easy for you. Ten thousand credits for the human," a gravelly voice said to my right. I shifted uncomfortably in my seat and held my glass to my lips, pretending to drink.

Taren didn't move and continued to stare at the two. He had one hand on the table and the other under it, no doubt gripping a weapon.

"Sure," Taren said.

The glass slipped out of my hand and clattered loudly on the table, its contents spilling across the metal surface. The soda sunk into the metal, drying up instantly. That would have amazed me in other situations.

"What?" I whispered, kicking Taren under the table and gripping my dagger tightly. I doubt I could win, but I sure as hell would try to take all three of them.

"Easy enough," one of the Vlarkan said. I felt its meaty hand latch onto my shoulder.

I got my dagger an inch out of the sheath before Taren said, "Wait."

The Vlarkan's grip on me loosened, but it still left its hand on my shoulder. Taren's hand was balled up in a fist on the tabletop and he looked like he was barely staying calm. He's just trying to catch them off-guard, right?

"Payment first," Taren said, unclenching his fist and holding out his wrist.

One of the Vlarkan muttered and ran his own wrist across Taren's as the credits transferred between the two of them. Once the transaction finished, Taren looked at the screen on his wrist with his crimson eyes and nodded.

"Good. We are done here," Taren said. The grip on my shoulder tightened and my mind went blank as the Vlarkan pulled me from the booth and forced me to stand.

I wanted to fight, to scream, to curse at Taren, but my body was frozen. To think I had trusted him and almost even wanted him.

We moved for the doorway and Taren shouted, "Hold on! One more thing."

Me and my new escorts turned around slowly to find Taren standing beside the table, taking another long swig of his molten drink before dramatically setting down the mug with a thud.

I couldn't even keep track of his movements. Everything happened in such a blur.

All I remember were two heavy thumps on either side of me, the smell of charred flesh, and Taren standing by the table with a gun that had green smoke trailing from the barrel.

I glanced at the two Vlarkan on either side of me, shuddering at the tidy holes in their foreheads with green smoke trickling out. Taren sat back down at the booth and motioned me over.

I felt like I was floating as I walked towards him and sat back down across from him. My brain was still in a fog and I wasn't completely sure what had just happened.

"Looks like they paid for several meals," Taren said with a grin.

"You sold me…" I muttered, not wanting to look him in the eye as I tried to process everything happening.

His grin faded, and he placed a hand on top of mine. I wanted to pull away from him, but the unnatural warmth pouring from his skin into mine was soothing.

My eyes met his as they flashed a vibrant purple and the heat on my hand increased.

"I may be a scoundrel, but I would never let anything bad happen to you. I will protect you. That much I promise," he said with so much confidence and sincerity that I believed it. "I do not have a choice anyway," he added, removing his hand and leaning back in his seat.

"What do you mean?" I asked, my mind fogging up again, but not out of confusion.

"That's for later conversations," he replied, looking towards the door by the bar as Zeth came out of it with two large plates. Her eyes cut to the Vlarkans on the floor and immediately snapped back to Taren, contorting into sheer frustration.

"What is this?" she asked, irritation weaved into her words as she dropped the heavy plates in front of us.

Taren shrugged, and I did the same when she looked at me for answers. *Don't look at me. I'm still at a loss for words.*

"This is exactly why you pay up front. Every damn time you come in here, I swear…" Zeth said.

"Can you get her another soda?" Taren asked, ignoring Zeth's fury.

She huffed and held out the glass pad for him to pay. He tapped the screen and added an extra five hundred credits.

"Never say I am not honest," Zeth said quietly. "You added a couple extra zeroes."

"No, I did not," Taren replied with a grin. "Sorry about the mess."

Zeth's entire demeanor changed in an instant, her scowl dissipating into a beaming and welcoming smile. "I will get that soda right out."

"Money really does let you get away with anything... wait... You just murdered those two people!" I said, reality finally gripping my mind.

"I thwarted a kidnapping," Taren said with a shrug.

I glanced over my shoulder at the two bodies on the floor and shuddered as I turned back toward Taren. "What would they have done with me?"

"Sold you to be some warlord's sex slave, probably," he replied off-handedly, picking up the fleshy tube from his plate and biting into it. It stretched and snapped like someone eating taffy.

My plate had the exact same thing on it. A tube the size of my arm that was colorless, except for the purple liquid seeping out of each end.

"What is this?" I asked, poking the tube with my finger, half expecting it to move. I was doing my best to ignore what he just said and try to move on, but fear, anger, desperation, panic, anxiety, and who knows what else was eating away at me. *At least there's plenty of stuff to distract me.*

CHAPTER SEVEN
TAREN

Abigail had been acting peculiar since I killed the Vlarkans. It made little sense to me why. She seemed to be upset that I killed them, and equally upset that I took their money first. They would have tried to kill me and taken her anyway, so I would have had to eliminate them, regardless. The money was just a nice bonus. *Perhaps, if I buy her some datapads, she will be happier. Maybe even a neurlin-relog.*

Abigail walked beside me, doing her best to keep pace with my long strides. I tried to slow down so she would not have to struggle, but breaking your normal pace is difficult unless you are focusing on it. I shortened my steps again, and she walked at a brisk pace beside me.

"Would you like to get some datapads to read about the different species?" I asked, glancing down at her. My body reacted as it did every time I looked at her now. A tingle that rolled through me from head to toe, urging me to let loose and mate with her.

I maintained control, and would not allow my biology to take over, but the Call of the Vreth was hard to resist, especially when it was sealed. She did not know what she did, but it did not matter to my body.

Her saliva contacting my skin imprinted her on me, further amplifying the feelings of desire I already had for her and forcing me to protect her at all costs. *I would have probably done that anyway, but now I do not have a choice.*

"Sure," she replied quietly. Another single word response. We were already almost back at the landing bay, and I still had not got her to speak to me fully.

"What is troubling you?" I asked, halting to the annoyance of the line of people behind me. They muttered under their breaths as they passed around me.

"I don't know, Taren. Probably the fact that I'm in an alien world with some criminal or whatever, and you just killed two people after trying to sell me. Not exactly a great start for me," Abigail replied not even remotely hiding her irritation.

Her hood was low over her face, but I could feel the animosity burning under it. "Plus, I'm hungry. All I've had to eat was alien eggs and some floppy dick thing that I couldn't even chew. I'm tired and hungry and sad and angry and confused and..."

I took her into my arms, pulling her tight against me as her shoulders heaved and liquid streamed down her face. I did not know if embracing was done by humans, but for Luranins, it was one of the few physical comforts we gave each other. The others being far more intimate.

"I'm sorry," she whispered after grunting against my chest for a few minutes. I could feel dampness where her face was and resisted the urge to wipe it away. "Thank you for saving me." She sniffled loudly and looked up at me. Her eyes were puffy and red, almost similar to a Luranin.

"I will always protect you," I said, leaving off the fact that I had to.

"Please, just warn me next time. I thought you really had sold me."

"Technically, I did sell you," I replied with a smirk.

"Taren... shhh," she said, burying her face against me for a few more seconds. "You're so warm."

Her body was cool against mine. My home planet was fiery and volcanic, leading to my species having a higher body temperature than most.

Feeling someone so much cooler against me was soothing and enjoyable. I placed my arms around her again and pulled her tightly against me, releasing her quickly when my skin shuddered and my viln hardened rapidly.

I can resist all I want, but there are some parts of my body that I cannot control.

An orange Bulra walked by, all of his eyes falling on Abigail and running up and down the length of her body through the gap in her cloak. Boiling hatred rose inside of me and I stepped in front of her, my face contorting into a snarl as I blocked his view of her body. His eyes met mine, and he changed to green as his body shrunk down and he hurried away.

I let out a sigh and turned to Abigail. *Also, some actions I cannot control it seems.*

"We need to get back, DX... Deborah will be back soon," I said, motioning for her to follow.

△△△

Deborah was already at the ship and waiting impatiently for us. For someone that did not have a face, she was excellent at displaying her emotions.

"I said two hours. It has been two and a half," Deborah said with displeasure.

"We were making some extra money," I replied with a shrug.

"Oh? How?"

"Taren sold me," Abigail chimed in quickly. She had a slight grin on her face and I was relieved to see that she was coming out of the odd mood she had been in since the Vlarkans.

Deborah's head tilted as she stared at me, waiting for an explanation. This was not the first time I had done similar things, and in my defense, they always worked out like I planned. Usually worked out like I planned. Once it did not work out like I had intended, but Deborah took care of it.

"Vlarkans," I said with a wink.

"Ah. Did you kill them?" Deborah replied knowingly.

"Yeah, he did," Abigail said. "I'm still a little mad that he did that without warning me."

"I did not have time to warn you," I said, glancing at Abigail apologetically. There was no actual regret for what I did, but it bothered me how she was reacting to it and making me feel a strange sense of guilt. *Call of the Vreth tugging at my central pilon.* I shook my head.

The Call of the Vreth really activated?

I nodded at Deborah. *Yep.*

It is incredible that you could resist it long enough to make that deal.

It was difficult.

"Taren has 'sold' me six times since we have been together," Deborah said to Abigail. "The Vlarkans are a miserable species and deserve what they get. He is," Deborah looked me over and continued in a sarcastic tone, "capable. You were never in any real danger."

"That's relieving at least," Abigail said with a sigh. "I'd just really like a heads up."

"Okay. If Vlarkans ask to buy you, I am going to say yes and then kill them. There's your warning," I said with a wink.

"Better than nothing. I guess," Abigail huffed.

"Anyway... Did you set up the meeting?"

"Yes. They are not on the station currently, but will be here by tomorrow. I left a communication token with their contact and they will inform us of the client's arrival," Deborah said.

What are you going to do about her?

Protect her, get through this deal, get back on the ship, then figure it out from there.

You will get worse until you mate with her. Perhaps it is best if we leave her on the ship and you stay away from her for the time being.

"No!" I roared, causing Abigail to jump away from me and Deborah to straighten up and stare me in the eye.

It is too late. Is it not?

I think so.

You should inform her.

We will pass through that jump-point when we get to it.

"Well. We have ten thousand credits to spend. Let's see what trouble we can get into," I said.

Abigail

It was a little relieving to hear that Taren had done that before and knew what he was doing. At least now I know what to expect if a Vlarkan offers to buy me. Taren did handily dispatch them... well, murder them. I keep being told how awful they are, but I'm not completely sold on the wanton killing of them. This is a whole different society, though, and I know nothing about it. All I can do is stick close to Taren and Deborah and hope for the best.

I was situated in between them as we walked down the streets, going off in a different direction than before. It was a little more relaxing now that I had a few hours to adjust to my surroundings.

There were still some aliens I saw that caught me off guard and terrified me, but I was mostly fine. It was unreal how quickly I got used to being somewhere so crazy. I guess that happens when you're thrust into it and spend hours immersed in it.

"Hey! You! In the cloak!" someone shouted at me from a storefront.

I glanced over at them and a small furry blue man was waving three of his hands at me wildly. The fourth hand was holding up what looked like a severed robot arm with wires dangling out the back as its limp wrist flopped around.

"Perfect size for you! Free installation!"

Deborah stared at the little blue man and her head moved with the flailing robot arm.

"It is an inferior model. I would not advise purchasing that upgrade," she said after a few seconds.

"Thanks?" I replied. "I don't want an *upgrade* right now, anyway."

"We can shop for them later. I know the best stores to buy upgrades and which ones are of the best quality."

"Okay..." I said, not knowing what else to say. I didn't particularly want any kind of robot parts. Although, the idea of it was cool.

"Not everyone is obsessed with replacing their flesh with metal," Taren said flatly.

"I am not obsessed. It is merely the most logical thing to do," Deborah replied. She sounded defensive.

"Sure," Taren said, filling the word with a lot of sarcasm for a single syllable.

The two remained quiet for a few moments before Taren muttered, "That's uncalled for. You do not have to be so rude."

"It was not rude. Just truthful," Deborah replied smugly.

"What did she say?" I asked, eager to join in the teasing. It was the first thing that's happened that I was actually familiar with.

"I informed him that..."

"No. Do not," Taren said sternly.

Deborah let out her rattling laugh. That had originally been off-putting for me, but I now found it endearing. "Fine."

"No, tell me," I insisted, but she kept silent. "Fine," I huffed.

"Here," Taren said as he paused in front of a dingy-looking store. The exterior was painted a sickly green, and the windows were either heavily tinted or filthy.

Judging by the stains on the sidewalk in front of it and on the door, the windows were just dirty.

"What is this?" I asked, not wanting to even step on the stained ground. It had crusty blotches of different colors, but they looked a lot like blood.

"I am going to continue on to the Detralu district," Deborah said, motioning down the street.

"That's fine," Taren replied, moving onto the dirty sidewalk in front of the store.

"I think I'll go with Deborah," I mumbled.

"No," Taren snapped, prompting me to step closer to Deborah. "The Detralu district is not the best place for a human to go to," he added quickly, his voice much calmer. "It would be safest if you stayed with me."

Deborah nodded slowly as I looked to her for direction. "I would suggest staying with Taren."

"Okay," I said, hesitantly moving towards

Taren.

I looked around for a sign or anything to hint what the store was, but the front of the two-story building was completely blank. My feet stuck to the sidewalk, and I cringed with each step I took as I joined Taren in front of the building.

Taren tilted his head at me as I stared at the building in disgust. "What's wrong?"

"This place looks nasty," I said, lifting my foot with a squelch before carefully placing it on a cleaner spot.

"It's the only shop that sells the ammunition for my weapon."

"Let's get this over with," I said.

The interior was nothing if not worse than the exterior. Everything looked sticky. The shelves lining the walls, the tables of weapons no display, the counter the shopkeeper was behind. Even the shopkeeper looked sticky.

I tucked my hands into my cloak, gripping it from the inside and holding it tightly against me. I didn't want any part of me to touch anything.

"Taren Lulart," the shopkeeper burbled from the counter. Her mouth had strands of sticky liquid that stretched with each word she spoke. She looked almost like a person dipped in honey, just with an extra set of eyes and a pair of ridges running up her bald head.

"Hello Liria," Taren said, leaning on the counter in front of her.

"Here for your usual?"

"Of course."

"Who's that with you?"

"My new apprentice."

"Teaching someone your ways, huh?" she giggled and waved at me. The honey-like substance dripped off her hand and before it touched the countertop, it flew back up to rejoin her body.

"Hi," I whispered, pulling my cloak even tighter.

"She's trustworthy," Taren said, glancing at me. "You do not have to be so mysterious."

"Okay," I replied, still keeping my cloak tightly against me. I wasn't trying to be mysterious. I just didn't want to touch anything. It seemed like that would be rude to say, so I moved up beside Taren and smiled at Liria.

"My, my. You are quite the pretty one. You sure she's just an apprentice?" Liria asked, closing all but one of her eyes.

Taren hesitated for a moment before grunting an acknowledgement.

"If you say so," Liria said, winking at me again. "He's quite a catch, you know?"

I felt my face burn hot and found something on the wall to look at. A massive curved blade was mounted on the wall. It looked bigger than anything even Taren could lift and had wiring running across the length of it. Two tubes filled with glowing green connected the handle to the blade.

"I'm going to look around," I said, waving at Taren to get his attention.

"Go ahead. Just keep an eye on the door," he said.

I moved into a nearby aisle, hesitant to wander too far from him. The store was small, but the station wasn't the safest place for me. Not until I knew what to watch out for, at least.

Two small boxes clattered loudly on the countertop as Livia continued to fish under the counter before dropping a third. "Three boxes?"

"That's fine," Taren said, holding out his wrist and completing the transaction. He pulled out his gun and replaced a canister in it with one from a box, then tucked the boxes into his coat. "Anything interesting happening?"

"Just the usual. A few Vlarkans on site, several Stravina…"

"Male or female?"

"Male."

"We will be sure to avoid them."

"Probably wise. Oh, there's a new species that I have not seen before," Livia said, her eyes lighting up under her thick coating of goo.

I picked up a few random items, turning them over in my hand but not looking at them as I eavesdropped on their conversation, peeking around a shelf. *Great, more people to avoid.* There were so many aliens that looked like they could tear me apart without breaking a sweat, but Taren said most of them were fine. It would take a while before I was used to not being nervous around everything twice my size with claws. *If I ever get used to that.*

"What does it look like?"

"It was wrapped in a cloak, so I am not sure. Almost twice your height, lanky, claws."

"A Cuvrun?"

"No, its hands had scales. Plus, it had six of them."

"Hands?"

"Yep."

"What is it?" I asked, my curiosity not allowing me to remain silent any longer as I rejoined them at the counter.

Taren motioned to me. "That's her favorite question."

Livia grinned. "No one I know is sure of what it is. It has not been seen in this galaxy before."

I watched Taren's body flex and move under his coat as he chatted with Livia, each word falling onto my deaf ears. Leaning on the counter, I felt a faint smile cross my face as he burst into laughter at something she said and glanced over at me, his eyes flashing to purple when they met mine. Something about him was alluring to me. The way he just went with the flow and didn't seem bothered by anything at all was refreshing.

Jason had always been overly worried about everything and rarely let me weigh in on anything or go anywhere alone. Even just to browse a store without him being right beside me.

The few times he asked my opinion, he just dismissed me with a hand wave and said I didn't have any real world experience. Well, now I have other world experience.

I giggled at myself; the sound made Taren immediately look at me again. The purple in his eyes became vibrant and deep as he approached me without a word, leaving Livia talking to empty air in front of her.

She sighed behind him and shook her head, muttering something along the lines of 'apprentice my asses.'

Taren stopped a few inches away from me, closing his eyes tightly as he placed a hand on my shoulder. I instinctively moved closer to him, craving to feel the heat of his body against me. Something deeper inside of me stirred, and I felt nervous suddenly.

"Don't mind me," I said, standing up straight and cringing as my cloak stuck to the counter.

Before I could move, Taren grabbed the edge of my cloak and freed it from its sticky prison. "Did you find anything you want?"

"Oh, I didn't know I could get anything. I don't know what any of it is, anyway."

"You get half of the money we made earlier. That's only fair," he said with a smirk, his eyes still purple.

"That makes sense. I think I'm good, though. Here, at least. I've got my stuff." I patted the weapons under my cloak.

"I know just the place to take you," Taren said, taking my wrist gently and pulling me towards the door.

"Oh, okay," I stammered, following behind him and trying not to think about his hand on me. I was getting far too worked up, and I had no idea why.

"Well, see you later. Thanks for coming," Livia said sarcastically as we stepped out of the doorway.

I waved quickly before the door closed.

"That was kind of rude, Taren," I said, trying not to laugh.

"What was?" he asked, releasing my wrist suddenly and looking away from me as his eyes turned blue.

"You just left mid-conversation?"

"Did I?"

"Yes? Are you okay?" I asked, suddenly alarmed. What if he was insane or something?

"I am fine," he said confidently, before clearing his throat. "Where were we headed?"

"You said you knew just the place to take me?"

"Oh." Taren exhaled loudly before staring pensively at the starry sky above us. "Right. Come on," he said finally, motioning for me to follow.

We walked for what felt like an hour before

I asked, "Is there not a bus or something?"

"Bus?"

"Like a vehicle. This place seems too big to walk the entire time."

"Ah. The underground light-wind system. Yes. It spans the entire city." Taren pointed at a large turquoise cylinder on one sidewalk in front of an alley. I had seen dozens of them but never thought to ask what they were. There were far stranger things on the station to ask about.

"Why don't we take that?" I asked. My legs were aching from walking for so long and I needed a break, but I was scared of sitting on another alien.

"It's not the safest location in the station," Taren said, staring at another turquoise cylinder as we passed.

"Neither was the restaurant you took me to," I countered. "Unless you want to carry me, we should use it."

Taren looked me up and down. I think he was seriously considering just carrying me the rest of the way.

"I was kidding about carrying me…"

"It would be no issue. You weigh nothing."

"Well, thanks," I said. I know it was probably not meant as a compliment, and in a world of huge muscular aliens was probably more of an insult, but I still appreciated it.

My feet left the ground suddenly, and I found myself cradled in Taren's arms. The heat from his body soothed me instantly, and I felt relieved to have my feet off the metal ground. I became so complacent that I almost didn't realize how embarrassing this was and let him carry me for several seconds before I said, "No, put me down."

I giggled once my feet touched the ground and slapped him gently on the arm. "You're silly."

"How so?" Taren asked, appearing to be genuinely confused. *I guess he really was just going to carry me.*

"Never mind. Let's take the light train, whatever. Please?"

"If you want. It certainly is much faster than walking," Taren said, approaching the nearest turquoise cylinder. The words 'light-wind entry' were painted in red at the top of the tall cylinder.

As soon as we stepped in front of it, the door opened to reveal a room that took up the entire interior of the massive cylinder. It was big enough for even the largest alien to get in.

Taren stepped on without hesitation and I joined him, gasping and feeling my knees go weak as I looked down and saw that the floor was transparent. *Why does every high up platform have to be transparent?*

I leaned against Taren and did my best to steady myself and look directly ahead into the street until the door closed and bathed us in darkness.

Distant lights illuminated the shaft below us, and I glanced down again before pushing tighter against Taren. His arm wrapped around me and he held me snuggly by his side as a light flickered on in the room.

"Are you well?" Taren asked, as he used his other hand to tap a pad on the wall.

"I'll be fine," I said, more to myself than him. "I just don't like heights, especially with nothing below me."

"There is a floor, though," Taren said, stomping his foot loudly.

"Please, don't."

"It will not break." He stomped again.

"I believe you," I said, staring forward and waiting for this to be over with.

The door in front of me slid open suddenly,

revealing a shimmering white tunnel that opened up into a massive room that was blindingly white.

Hundreds of aliens mingled with one another, most of them crowded against a green metal wall. Small booths and kiosks lined the walls, with small tunnels like ours dotted between them.

"How did we get here?" I asked, following Taren out of the cylinder.

"We were just on the grav-lift? You were complaining about the floor?"

"I know," I said, shaking my head. "I didn't feel us move."

"Why would you feel a grav-lift move?"

"You know what? Never mind. What is this?"

"One of the light-wind stations. Have you not been listening this entire time?"

"I know... okay. Whatever," I said with a giggle. "What do we do?"

"Wait for the next light-wind."

"What is a light-wind?"

"A transportation system."

"You do this on purpose, don't you?"

Taren grinned and didn't answer my question. I glimpsed his pearly white teeth and the way his face lit up caused my heart to beat faster.

"It will separate us, in the light-wind. Wait for me when we get there, okay?" Taren said as we stepped into the group of aliens near the green wall.

"Okay," I replied quietly. I didn't like the sound of that. Getting separated from him or Deborah was the last thing I wanted right now. I couldn't believe that just a few hours ago, I was debating on staying here and figuring things out on my own.

I liked Deborah from the start, but Taren was another story. He pissed me off at first, but the longer I'm with him, the more I'm seeing the appeal.

"Where are we going, anyway?" I asked as the line shifted forward. It was moving a lot faster than I would have thought. The group of aliens were divided into lines and there were a good fifty in front of me before.

When the green wall opened, at least half of them went through, stepping into the bright green light.

"It is a surprise," Taren said, walking beside me as our line dwindled again. We were next.

"What is it?"

"A surprise is… when you take someone

somewhere unexpected, or give..."

"I know what a surprise is," I said, shaking my head. "I mean, what's the surprise?"

"It would not be one if I told you."

"Whatever, Taren," I said with a grin. It felt like I was on a date more than being on an alien planet with a criminal that was trying to sell stuff on a black market. I actually had to remind myself of that to keep myself grounded sometimes. *At least he's cute and charming... in a weird way.*

CHAPTER EIGHT
TAREN

I did not want to be down here, but Abigail seemed intent on using the light-wind, and I did not want to keep her from experiencing what she wanted. My head stayed on a swivel as we waited for the light-wind to open. I chose a higher floor of the system. It gets seedier the further down you go, but it still was unpatrolled by the station security.

QT-314 was far too large to patrol thoroughly. A lot of areas had fallen to different organizations that maintained strangleholds over them, or worse, had fallen into complete anarchy where anything goes.

The light-wind system fell into the latter category. Station security was kill-on-sight on deeper levels, but on the higher levels we should be fine.

The green wall in front of us slid open, bathing us in the green glow of the light-wind. Abigail hesitated before stepping in, looking back at me for encouragement. I motioned for her to step through, patting her on the shoulders with both my hands.

With a quick flash of light, she was gone, and I followed behind her.

A tingle ran across the length of my body as my vision was overtaken by green. The tingle turned into violent vibrations, rattling me down to my bones before suddenly vanishing and leaving me completely senseless except for the blinding green in my sight.

The bright green faded to a haze as the next station appeared in front of me and I stepped out of the light-wind, tripping over something below me and toppling to the ground. My skin reacted instantly, coating me in stone as I hit the metal floor with a ringing thud.

"Shit, sorry," Abigail said, jumping to her feet and offering me a hand.

I took it carefully and allowed her the guise of helping me up. If I had actually tried to support myself with her, she would have surely fallen on top of me. My body rippled at the thought of her body lying on top of mine and I half-wished I had pulled her onto me.

Before I could stand, a Bithra came through the light-wind, meeting a similar fate to me as she tripped over Abigail. All of her eyes went wide as her tentacles flailed wildly for anything to grasp, the light of the light-wind no doubt clouding her vision.

I gripped Abigail's hand tightly, yanking her on top of me just as one of the Bithra's thick tentacles slammed through the air where her head had just been. She landed with her ass squarely on my viln before falling against my torso; her cloak flailed open and gave me a clear view of her bust as it squished against me in its leather wrapping.

My viln reacted instantly, throbbing and desperate to be free from its bindings. I forced myself to take a deep breath and wrapped my arms around Abigail as I backed away from the Bithra before it came toppling to the ground.

Flipping Abigail to the ground beside me, I leapt to my feet and pulled her up before hurrying away from the light-wind exit as a Sasquatar stepped out of the light-wind and tripped over the writhing Bithra.

"Sorry!" Abigail shouted over her shoulder as I threw an arm around her and rushed us to the exit.

Once we were back topside Abigail said, "My bad. I felt sick when I got off whatever that was and I thought I was going to throw up. I wasn't thinking."

"It's disorienting the first time," I consoled her. "Most times, actually. Next time, make sure to keep moving. That Bithra almost took your head off."

Abigail winced and asked, "Are they bad, too?"

"What? No. They are just large, strong, and easily startled."

She made a thoughtful noise, and leaned into me as we walked down the street, my arm still across her shoulder. I had originally placed it there to help usher her out of the light-wind, but now it felt right to leave it. I was not sure why it brought me joy, but it did, and Abigail seemed to be appreciative.

"Well, thanks for saving me... again," she said, putting an arm around my waist and squeezing me.

"You are welcome," I replied, trying not to think about the proximity of her hand to my already aroused viln. The sensations of pressure from her ass still lingered and made it hungry for more. The pocket in my pants was the only thing keeping it contained at that moment.

We walked for several minutes before the store came into sight. I maneuvered us across the street toward it, and Abigail tilted her head at the display in the window as we approached.

"Neurlin-relogs?" she asked, craning her neck to meet my eyes.

"I think you will enjoy it," I said, hoping I was right. She was so full of questions, and this seemed the best place to get her answers. Some answers, at least.

ABIGAIL

"At least it's cleaner than that other place," I said, smiling at Taren, his eyes flashing purple.

This section of the station was much nicer than the first one we went into. It was also a lot more uniform. The buildings were all the same shape and size, with the same shiny white exterior. Likewise, the road and sidewalk were much cleaner and shiny.

The strange bench-like creatures were more numerous here, too, and several armed aliens in white uniforms were positioned up and down the street with large guns in hand. It also had far fewer people walking around.

SO I ACCIDENTALLY BECAME AN AL...   125

"I should hope it's clean," Taren replied, leading us through the doorway.

He didn't seem like the type to walk down the street holding someone, but I'm happy he is. It feels right and I'm enjoying the heat radiating off of him. How he didn't sweat constantly while wearing that coat was beyond me.

The inside of the store was completely white with what looked like massage chairs of varying sizes spread across the floor. A single woman... I think... was at the center of the room and I'm pretty sure she smiled at us when we stepped in. The rest of the store was empty. No shelves, no tables, no merchandise.

"Greetings and welcome," the woman said warmly, her voice feminine and silky. She was hard to look at, almost like she was blurry, but I could get a vague sense of what she looked like.

"Hello," I said with a small wave as Taren motioned for me to go ahead.

"My name is Bitruscinaya, but you may call me Bit," the woman said. "What are you interested in today?"

"Hi Bit," I said. "I'm Abigail. Um... I don't even really know what this place is." I glanced over at Taren and he nodded at me before sitting on one of the larger massage chairs by the door.

"Well, Abigail, let me show you some of our wares and you can decide what you would like then."

"Sure."

"I was thinking of a species compendium," Taren said, watching the door intently.

"Oh. That is an excellent choice. It helps to know who or what you are dealing with." Bit smiled and waved her hand across one of the blank walls. A thin white panel slid down and revealed hundreds of small slits with the handles of peculiar devices sticking out of them.

Bit grabbed one of the handles and pulled out the device, giving me a clearer view of it. It looked like a very long needle with a small blinking box attached to the base, just above the handle. I didn't particularly like where this was going.

"Um, what is this?" I asked, feeling my eyes widen as she presented the needle to me.

"A neurlin-relog," Bit tilted her head at me before looking at Taren. "You seem to know about this. Did you not inform her of what we do here?"

"I wanted it to be a surprise," Taren said with a shrug.

"Ah. Very well. So, this," she said, pointing at the tip of the needle. "Goes into the base of your brain connection. It is sterilized, do not worry."

"That's not even what I'm most worried about," I said, chuckling nervously. *Why did he think this was a good surprise?*

"The information is uploaded into the brain of your choosing. Within thirty seconds you will have full access to everything contained within," Bit continued, finishing with a smile. "Any questions?"

"Several..." I said, my mind going blank at the thought of that needle being shoved into my brain. The idea that I could have all of this information injected into my brain was amazing, but the process left a lot to be desired.

Bit stared at me expectantly for a few seconds before saying, "Well, I will answer the most common ones. It does not affect your reproductive capabilities. If you have a grulwig sac, it will not affect its capability to produce. The file contains five thousand two hundred and thirty-seven entries. It does not have information on the Vulrax system. And it will not change your vision. Does that answer everything?"

"Um... Does it hurt?"

"It will not injure you."

"Okay, but is it painful?"

"Not at all," she replied cheerfully, motioning toward a chair. "Lie down here. I will collect payment and then we will install this."

"Oh, right, money."

"I will pay for it," Taren said, standing up and joining us as I situated myself in the chair.

"Face down please," Bit said.

I rolled over and placed my face in the center hole.

"That will be nine thousand twenty-three credits." *That's so expensive, or is it?* I didn't really know how much stuff cost here yet, but it sounded pricey. I heard a few clicks and chimes before Bit said, "Thank you. We will begin now. Please remain still."

I gritted my teeth and tried to distract myself from the fact that the large needle was probably moving towards me at that very moment.

My breathing became shallow, and I wanted to leap up and run out the door, but I was too scared that I would just end up stabbing myself in the back of the head with the needle if I even flinched.

Something warm and wet ran across the back of my neck, soothing me in an instant. My entire body went limp, and I felt completely fine. All thought of fear and running dissipated in an instant and I felt the slightest pressure push into the base of my neck.

I could feel the needle as it pressed deeper inside of me, but it didn't hurt. It almost tickled. An itch that was impossible to scratch.

My mind went completely blank as I passed out.

△△△

It felt like I had been asleep for hours when my eyes fluttered open. I was turned over and creeping upright as the chair switched positions with a quiet whir. I let out a gasp when I saw a mechanical face with glowing green eyes in front of me and started to scream for Taren, but Bit lifted the mask from her face and smiled at me.

"All done! You should have access to the data shortly," she said, setting the mask in a cubby on the wall and depositing the needle into a hole.

"How long was I out?" I asked groggily. I was worried I made Taren miss his meeting. Although, I'm sure he would have just gone without me.

"Ten seconds," Bit replied cheerfully.

"Seriously?"

"Yes?"

"It felt like a lot longer," I said, rubbing the back of my neck. Sensations were returning, and it felt a little sore.

"That's the effect of the anesthesia," Bit said with a shrug. I peeked around her. Taren was still sitting by the door, watching it intently.

"I couldn..." My mind suddenly became flooded. Images and information. Sounds, smells, touch. I slammed my eyes shut and screwed up my face, trying to settle my racing thoughts. "What's happening?" I asked. I'm pretty sure I actually screamed it.

"Hang in there, it is almost over," Bit replied. A hand landed on my shoulder and squeezed it gently.

Suddenly. My mind cleared and I could think clearly again. I slowly opened my eyes and looked at Bit. "You're a Balyys?"

Bit clapped happily. "Yes! Good, it looks like the information has integrated successfully. It took it a second longer than it should have, and I was mildly concerned."

"What happens if it doesn't integrate?"

"Some things just get fried. Less than five percent. It is no concern," she said, waving a hand to dismiss the question.

"Okay..."

"What am I?" Taren asked, leaving his post and standing over me.

"Luranin. Your women are terrifying," I said as images flashed in my mind of their rituals and capabilities. The women were battle-hungry and loved a fight. The men, thankfully, appeared to be more laid back.

"That they are," Taren said with a smirk. "Now you can quit asking me 'what is that' constantly."

"I guess I can, huh?" I giggled. "Thank you, Bit."

"My pleasure. Be sure to sleep soon so your brain can reorganize the information and prevent you from becoming overwhelmed. Return anytime!" she said as we walked out into the street.

My mind raced as we walked through the street. If we had been in the busier sector from before, I think my head would have exploded. Every time we walked past a new alien, information popped into my head and ran through facts about them. It was disjointing, suddenly knowing all of this, and my mind wasn't sure how to handle it yet.

Much to Taren's frustration, I found a way to cope.

"Cuvrun."

"Bustia."

"Sasquatar."

"Krung."

"Yetal."

"Preth."

I listed off the name of every species we passed.

"Are you going to continue to do that?" Taren asked after the tenth alien I listed.

"Probably. It's helping me keep my brain steady," I replied. "Ceqal."

Taren sighed. "I would almost rather have you question me."

"Too late now! This is great, though. Thank you!" I said happily, leaning into him and giving him a hug. His arms immediately wrapped around me and squeezed me tightly, pulling me into the pocket of heat he had trapped under his coat. I just wanted to fall asleep in there.

"I am glad to hear it's pleasing you. We need to find you a place to sleep."

"Can we just go back to the ship?"

"I would not risk it. We would have to pass through much larger crowds and it might harm your brain. We can get a room in this sector."

"It seems kind of fancy here, you already spent a lot on me. I think? I don't know how your money works." *It was almost the price of buying a human, though. Maybe the Vlarkans were just cheaping out.*

"Normally, I would agree, but the risk of injury to your mind is not worth saving the credits," Taren replied after some consideration. "There is an inn over there we can stay at. We should still have several hours before the meeting."

"Works for me," I replied absently. My mind was too busy going over the dozen different species sitting outside a restaurant.

Taren ushered me across the street as I continued mumbling species names, and led me into a dazzling lobby. Everything was glistening gold except for the shiny white floors. Our footsteps echoed loudly in the massive room as we approached a desk with a small furry creature in a shiny golden jumpsuit.

Its nose twitched as we approached and its ears followed us as we walked through the lobby. It only looked up from what it was doing when we stopped in front of the desk. The creature looked almost like a massive rat, but it had a human-like nose and mouth, which was very unsettling.

"Treglon..." Taren clamped his hand over my mouth before I could finish saying the word, and the Treglonical glared at me silently before looking at Taren.

"What do you need?" it asked with a shockingly deep voice.

"Just a room for a few hours," Taren said, leaving his hand over my mouth. I resisted the urge to lick him again.

"We are not that kind of inn. Go to the Prolo sector if you need to rent by the hour," the Treglonical said, returning to the pad in its hands. It looked like it was playing a game.

"She just got a neurlin-relog and needs to sleep."

"Ah. Apologies. You two do not look like the type that can afford a nerulin-relog," the little rat said bluntly. "Eight hours should be sufficient for most species and that will be fifteen hundred credits." It looked Taren up and down, glanced at me, then back to Taren. "Paid up front."

Taren grunted in annoyance and held out his wrist, keeping his other hand over my mouth.

"What was that for?" I asked as we climbed a set of stairs at the rear of the lobby that led to a grav-lift.

"Their species' name is a very nasty insult to them," he replied, glancing over his shoulder.

"Seriously? Why?"

He shrugged. "That's just how it is. They get

aggressive when someone uses it."

"It was just a little rat thing. How bad could it be?" I asked. Not that I wanted to offend anyone, but it didn't seem like something he would be concerned with. My mind dredged up the information on the Treglonicals and I said, "Oh." They apparently get much larger when angered. Much, much larger.

Our room was pleasant and had a lot of features to it, but the decor was incredibly sparse and everything was the same shiny gold as the lobby, even the bedding. The floor was black instead of white, and the room was huge with a massive bed in the center.

Two windows were on the wall opposite the door and gave a view of the street and people passing by. Taren immediately hit a console by the window and they tinted until they were completely opaque.

Another door led to a bathroom with the weirdest assortment of objects in it. I was assuming they were toilets? They all had the vague shape of a toilet, but most of them looked like the drawings of a two-year-old. At least I hoped they were toilets, because I took the liberty of using one. There were six in total, a sink, and a giant open space that had a glass door on it.

After poking around the room, I sat on the

bed and looked at Taren as he sat on a gold couch in the corner. "What are you going to do while I sleep?" I asked.

Taren shrugged and looked around the room. "I will probably bathe and wander the area. You will be safe here."

"Sure, okay," I said, leaning back onto the soft bed and sighing deeply as it enveloped me in comfort. It just dawned on me that I hadn't slept in over twenty-four hours.

A deep yawn escaped my lips as I scooted further onto the bed, rolling around as I undid my cloak. As soon as the clasp unlatched, it disappeared from my hands, sinking back into my suit.

I would have thought that was amazing, but I was suddenly far too tired to even think about it. As soon as my head hit the pillow, before I could even get under the blanket, I was out.

CHAPTER NINE
ABIGAIL

I awoke from the best sleep I had ever had, feeling more rejuvenated than I had in who knows how long. My brain also seemed to cooperate and wasn't bombarding me with information any longer.

The room was dim, but I could still barely see, and I glanced around for Taren. I was a little disappointed to find him gone, but he had told me he might wander.

"Guess I'll just hang out in the room," I muttered, climbing out of bed and stretching.

I paced around the room, looking over some of the strange objects in it and trying to puzzle out what they did. Most of them looked like they had a function and just weren't decorative, but I couldn't for the life of me figure them out.

Turning a small cube over in my hand, I pressed a button hidden seamlessly in a corner and it illuminated, glowing a bright yellow light. *Curiouser and curiouser.* I flipped it over and searched for any markings, but stopped when I heard a quiet grunting coming from the bathroom.

Gripping the cube tightly, I walked over to the door and placed my ear against it. The grunting sounded pained, and it sounded like Taren.

"Taren? Are you in there?"

"Just a minute," he replied hastily, the sound of agony in his voice.

"Are you hurt? What happened?"

"What? No, I am fine."

Something slammed loudly in the bathroom and worried that he fell over and passed out from an injury. I opened the door, dropping the cube on the ground at the display before me.

Taren had his hand planted on the wall, and his other hand firmly gripping the largest cock I had ever seen.

"What are you doing? I said I am fine!" he said in a panic.

I closed the door quickly. It slid from the ceiling, hit the cube on the ground, and opened again.

"Go!" Taren said, turning his back to me and quickly gathering his clothes scattered around the floor. My face turned beet-red as his ass was on full display before me and his cock was dangling between his legs.

"Sorry!"

The door came down again, hit the cube, and re-opened.

"Why didn't you lock the door?" I asked in a panic.

"Move the damn lamp!" Taren shouted, doing his best to cover himself.

I hastily grabbed the cube, which was apparently just a lamp, and retreated to the bed as the door closed.

Taren stepped out of the bathroom fully clothed a few moments later, glancing over at me.

"You know I could have…"

Taren opened the door and stepped into the hallway, closing it quickly.

"Helped you with that," I whispered to myself.

Letting out a sigh, I fell back onto the bed. *It was probably for the best. I probably shouldn't be sleeping with aliens, right?*

Are you trying to mate with Taren?

Deborah? My heart started racing at the sudden intrusion into my very private thoughts.

It is fine if you are. I was just curious.

Where are you? I did my best to change the subject.

In the hotel's lobby. Which room are you in? Taren is not replying to me.

I scrambled around the room, looking for any sign of the room number, finally finding it engraved on a metal plate under a small screen by the door.

232b.

A couple of minutes later, a chime sounded in the room and the small screen illuminated, showing Deborah standing in the hallway. The screen blacked out as it switched to another display. It still showed Deborah but gave some kind of x-ray view, and I could see the inner-workings of her body. She really was mostly a machine, but I could still see some things inside of her that looked like organs, including a brain. She also had a ridiculous amount of blades stored inside of her.

I tapped a green button on the screen, and the door slid open.

"Hello," Deborah said, stepping in and looking around the room. "This is unlike Taren."

"I had to go somewhere to sleep so my brain

wouldn't explode or something?"

"Why would your brain explode?"

"I got a neural something thing, and I know all about a bunch of alien species now!" I said excitedly, trying to think of what Deborah was, but coming up empty. Maybe the augmentations were too much for me to figure out.

"Neurlin-relog?"

"Yeah, that."

"You only need to sleep within eight hours. There was plenty of time to return to the ship or a less costly sector. Very peculiar," Deborah said, peeking into the bathroom.

I felt a little warm and fuzzy at the thought of Taren bringing me somewhere nice when he didn't have to. *Then again, he might not have known that I had eight hours.*

"Taren has had neurlin-relogs before, he knows," Deborah stated.

Aw, he's just being nice to me. Now I felt even more upset about missing my window to seduce him. *Maybe there will be another opportunity soon.*

"For what?" Deborah asked.

"Can you stop doing that?"

"No."

"How does Taren deal with this?"

"I do not know. It would drive me insane if I could not control when I broadcast. He has dealt with it for six cycles at this point. Perhaps you should ask him for tips," Deborah teased.

"Cycles?"

"It would calculate to three Earth years. Two point seven eight nine three two, to be exact."

"How did you two meet?" I asked. I never even thought about how long they'd been doing this or how they met. They seem like an odd-pairing, but they get along so well.

"Taren rescued me. I was just a sprout, born into slavery at a Vlarkan colony. They augmented me to make me grow faster and give me strength so I could work in their mines," Deborah said, pausing to reflect.

"I'm so sorry…"

"Do not be. It is in the past. Taren found me while stealing a shipment of Vexil ore from the colony. I had hidden inside a crate for a quick nap and awoke on the ship. I thought for sure he was going to launch me out of the airlock. The Vlarkans would have," Deborah laughed. "Instead, he offered me a spot in his crew. I was always adept with technology, so learning a starship was nothing."

"So all these augmentations you have, they did to you?"

"No, I was actually quite fond of the strength they provided me. So I continued to add them. With enough of them, I would never be a slave again. So far, it has turned out as I imagined," she replied with a sigh. "It is hard to believe Taren took me in twenty cycles ago. My life changed forever because of him, and I am eternally grateful."

"I thought you said it had been six cycles?"

"Oh, that is just how long I have had the neural-link," Deborah chuckled. "Where has Taren gone to? Did you try to mate with him and he fled?"

"You are very forward," I said, shaking my head. "No. He left quickly."

After I saw him masturbating in the bathroom.

"Ah, a favorite past-time of his."

"Okay, Deborah." I giggled and felt my face heat as I re-envisioned the scene from earlier ending with Taren inside of me. *I really wish I could have taken advantage of that. It's too bad he got embarrassed and stormed out.*

Deborah tilted her head and remained silent for a moment before saying, "Taren is still nearby. He just replied to me finally."

"Is he coming back?" I asked, feeling a little excited to see him.

"It took some threats, but yes," Deborah said, marching toward the door.

"What threats? Why?" I asked, following her into the hallway.

"Wait here."

"Where are you going?"

"To another sector. Taren will... fetch you momentarily."

"Back to being cryptic again?"

"Yes."

With that, Deborah disappeared into the grav-lift at the end of the silver hallway. I leaned against the doorframe and sighed. *Why are these two always so complicated?*

TAREN

I will tell her what has happened if you do not return here.

I pinched the bridge of my nose and waved at the bartender to pay my tab. The first place I have been to that did not make me pay up front.

You have ten seconds to respond.

I am coming. Freknal, Deborah, calm down.

She is waiting for you in the room.

I left the grav-lift on our floor and trudged to the room, trying to figure out the best way to tell Abigail about her marking me. It was not something I had experienced before.

Like every other Luranin male, they warned me from a young age about allowing someone's mouth near your palm, and I always kept it closely guarded. Our women were more... daring than most species and were fond of taking what they wanted. So, you had to be on guard whenever around them.

Things with Abigail feel different from the stories I have heard. It's almost like I want this more than just the Call of the Vreth demanding it. She had always had an allure to her, even back on Earth in the grocery store.

I needed to tell her. I did not know exactly what I was feeling for her, but if this was all just the bond, I wanted to remain companions. She seemed to enjoy being out here with us, and I would welcome her aboard the ship as a crew-member.

The bond is only in effect until you mate, then the male's mind is freed several hours later. I worried that if that happened, I would lose all interest in her beyond being a traveling companion and she would not take it well.

On the other side, if we do not mate, I will eventually become consumed with desire and be unable to function properly until we do.

I sighed at the door to our room, staring at it and hoping for it to enlighten me with the answer to my concerns. It remained silent as I pushed it open and stepped into the room.

"Greetings," I said, immediately regretting my choice of words as Abigail tilted her head at me. She was sitting on the bed, leaning back on a pile of pillows. If I did not know better, I would have thought she was being suggestive.

I felt a tremor run through my body as my skin rippled. Her skin-tight leather outfit did nothing but amplify her appeal and reveal every exquisite curve. Being hidden under the leather added a small layer of mystery that did nothing but make my viln throb.

Steeling myself, I tore my gaze away as she shimmied to the edge of the bed, leaning on her knees and displaying her ample breasts. The connectors on her suit had come undone, and I could clearly see her cleavage.

My viln ached again, demanding I look, but I walked over to a wall and pretended to mess with the temperature console. *Wish I got to finish what I was doing earlier. This would be easier to resist.*

"About earlier..." Abigail said, humming quietly as she trailed off.

"It was not my fault you barged in. I should have locked the door, but you should have knocked," I said defensively. Deborah observed everything on the ship, much to my chagrin, but she never came into a room unannounced.

"Oh. Yeah. Sorry about that. I was just wondering though..." she said, making that humming noise again.

"What?" I felt put on the spot and prepared myself to retort whatever she said.

"Did you finish?" Abigail asked confidently after a few seconds of silence.

"Did I finish...?" I was at a loss for words. Whatever preparations my mind had done were woefully under equipped for such a direct question.

"Mhmm."

I glanced over at her and she locked eyes with me, fumbling with the connectors on her suit. Another one popped open and her tits pushed the leather apart further, almost spilling out of the opening. "Whoops," she said with a sly grin.

"What is happening?"

"Taren Lulart, are you that dense?"

"I can turn my body to stone," I replied off-handedly.

Abigail giggled, and another ripple rushed across me. "That's not what I meant, silly."

She stood up and sauntered over to me, pressing her body against mine and burying her face in my chest. My arms moved of their own accord, wrapping around her and squeezing her tightly into me.

The coolness of her body washed into me, sending a mixture of relaxation and desire spreading throughout me as my skin rippled once again.

"It took me a minute," she said, rubbing her cheek against my chest.

"What did?"

"Piecing together what Deborah was doing."

"What was Deborah doing?"

Her hands slipped further down my back, glided across my waist, and dipped down between us, across my thighs. My viln could sense her closeness to it and fidgeted, desperate to feel her touch.

"Your eyes are so vibrant right now," Abigail said, staring up at me. "The most beautiful indigo I've ever seen."

I closed my eyes and tried to will myself to calm down. My body and mind desperately craved what she was offering, but I needed to inform her of the Call of the Vreth before we did anything.

I was making progress until Abigail's hand planted itself firmly onto my viln. A grunt escaped my lips, and I snapped my eyes open again. Abigail wasn't looking into my eyes anymore. She was staring at the ever-growing bulge in my pants, her hands no longer on it, but still inches away.

My viln throbbed and struggled, trying to escape the pocket I tucked it into.

"What is going on in there?" Abigail asked, her eyes wide as my viln shifted visibly. It had grown large enough to leave a distinct outline on my pants as it shifted.

All thoughts of being subtle had been thrown from the cargo bay when she grabbed me.

"My viln craves you. It aches and throbs for you," I whispered, giving into the Call and undoing my pants. They slipped from my waist and fell to the floor, my viln popping into full view as it thickened even further in the cool air of the room.

It swung around, bending as it searched

blindly for Abigail, desperate to feel her cool skin against it. She stared at it thoughtfully for a few moments before reaching out and gripping its base. It went rigid as she ran her hand along its length and a ripple of stone crossed my body again. Her cool grip on my viln was perfect, and the softness of her hands as they stroked its shaft almost made my mind go blank.

Abigail pressed against me, keeping a firm hand on my viln as she craned her neck to me, puckering her lips out and closing her eyes. I was not familiar with what she wanted and imitated her. Some strange form of human mating, I supposed. It was honestly rather arousing.

Abigail giggled when she opened her eyes, releasing my viln and grabbing me around the neck with both hands, pulling my face down to meet hers and pressing her lips into mine.

Something inside of me snapped at the feeling of her cool lips against the heat of mine. Our mouths glided across one another frantically, her tongue flitting into my mouth and dancing with my tongue. The slippery sensations caused my viln to flail in search of her body, slapping her lightly on her waist. She dropped one of her hands, gripping it again.

Pressure built inside of me. Pounding, pulsing, aching. My body wanted to release it, but I held strong as my own hands worked their way down

Abigail's body, the leather of her outfit squeaking quietly as they passed and finally settled on her ass, gripping each cheek tightly and squeezing as I lifted her into the air. Her legs wrapped around my waist and she pulled herself tightly against my body as our mouths explored the other's.

I fell back onto the bed with a quiet thud and Abigail on top of me. My viln slipped under her ass, wiggling its way into the space between us.

Abigail pressed against it, sliding it between her legs and rubbing herself across its length as she undid the remaining connectors on her suit, shrugging it off her shoulders and revealing her smooth skin.

My eyes wandered her body hungrily, not knowing where to look first. Darting from her tits to her waist, to her eyes, to her mouth as she flicked a tongue out and stood up.

She wiggled above me, her tits bouncing with each movement as she slipped her leather suit over her hips and down to her ankles.

She wavered for a moment, but I caught her by the waist and steadied her before she fell over.

"Thanks," she giggled, kicking off the rest of her suit and standing above me in all her glory. I felt ravenous looking over her body and was relieved to see a delicious mound between her legs. I had not known what to expect from a human body, but I knew what that was.

Sitting up, I gripped her thighs firmly, running my hands along them as I approached the folds between her legs, pausing just before touching them. Testing the waters, I slipped a finger between them, lightly running it across the length of her slit and relishing the sound escaping from her lips as I hit a small fleshy bump at the front. Her voln was swollen, and she pressed firmly against my finger as it worked its way back to it.

Her scent was intoxicating. The Call of the Vreth heightened my senses. I could smell her depths and craved them more than anything.

My viln wanted access immediately, but it would have to wait. I gripped the smooth skin of her waist, and pulled her to her knees, directly into my mouth.

The taste was indescribable. I found myself lost in her depths, relishing each movement of my tongue and the feeling of my hands running across the smooth skin of her back before settling on her thick ass.

Her own hands groped behind her, desperately searching for my impatiently waiting viln, but her arms were too short to do more than graze its head, which did nothing but make it throb.

She gave up quickly as I pressed my tongue against her own throbbing voln, sucking on it lightly and savoring every taste. I flitted across it, adding more and more pressure until her breathing became erratic and she gripped my horns tightly, pulling my head tightly against her body.

Her knees tightened around my head, squeezing me and sending me further into the depths of ravenous hunger as I lapped at her greedily. It was as if this was the last sustenance in the universe and I had not eaten in weeks.

Abigail's gasps turned to a long moan, and she breathed, "Keep doing that, don't stop."

I followed her orders to the letter, maintaining the rhythm I had developed and hungrily devouring her core. Everything felt right. Like I knew my exact place in the universe and I was whole.

Giving her pleasure brought me immense happiness, the likes of which I had never experienced, and I wished it would never end.

Abigail moaned loudly again and quivered on top of me, her knees tightening against my head as she lifted herself off my face. I tried to lean up and follow her, still desperate for more, but she held my head down by the horns.

"No, no. Wait, ah, ah," she said before losing her words and convulsing. The tremble of her hands ran through my horns and into my head. I felt like I was there with her, feeling what she felt.

She hovered over me, panting wildly before finally catching her breath. Her face broke out into a grin and she slipped off of me, lying on her side beside me, shifting and making a pouty face as she pressed her tits against me.

The sight of them squishing against my body made my viln flail again, and she gripped it quickly, stroking it and soothing it, giving in to its demands for her touch.

Abigail slipped further down my body, running her hands up my shirt and groping me greedily as her face made its way to my viln. She took its head into her mouth and it pressed itself further inside without warning. Abigail didn't relent, though.

She gripped it tightly and whispered, "No, sir. I'm in charge," before taking the head back into her mouth.

I could feel the cool slipperiness of her tongue as it ran around the head and she pushed it deeper into her mouth.

My viln tried to take control again, but she squeezed it tightly, keeping it under control and licking the base of its head. I watched with wide eyes, anxious to see every detail, as my head disappeared into her mouth again.

The sensations were indescribable and unlike anything I had ever experienced.

The pressure building inside me grew exponentially with each movement she made, finally retreating to a tolerable level as she pulled my viln out of her mouth, sucking on the head and releasing it with an audible pop.

"Behave yourself," she whispered to my viln before climbing on top of me and maneuvering it to line up with her folds.

It did not need any guidance. As soon as her body was within reach, it dove inside of her. Abigail let out a gasp that twisted into a moan as it wiggled its way to her depths, her walls squeezing it at every possible point. She raised up and lowered down on it slowly, but it took over and drove itself deep inside of her.

I sat up, pulling her tightly against me and running my hands through her hair before gliding them down her back and breathing in her scent again. A tingle ran through my body and my skin rippled, the stone traveling across my body and stopping on my lower back.

I wrapped an arm around her waist, pulling her even closer to me as I worked my way between her thighs and found her voln again.

She was dripping wet, and it slipped into her slit with ease, caressing her voln as my viln dove deeper and deeper into her, wiggling wildly with each movement. Her breathing became frantic again, and this time, I joined in.

Unable to control myself, I let out a groan and planted my free hand on the back of her head, pulling her face to my chest as the pressure built to an unbearable level inside of me.

She was damp with sweat and it gave me a strange sense of satisfaction that sent me closer to losing control. I wished I had removed my shirt and could feel her against my skin, but it was too late now.

Abigail quivered on my viln and against my finger, each movement making her gasp and moan, each movement making my viln thicken and tremble.

Electric chills prickled every inch of my skin and another ripple crossed my body as the stone at my lower back launched out, wrapping around both of our waists and trapping Abigail against me, and my hand against her voln. The stone-purchase ensured a successful mating.

She either didn't notice or didn't care as she buried her face into my chest, her muffled moans music to my ears and pushing me over the edge. My viln went rigid, pulsating wildly as it readied itself for release.

Abigail gasped. "No, no. I can't. I can't. It's too much," she said, trying to pull off of me, her words getting lost in another loud moan escaping her lips. She pushed against me, but my stone-purchase had locked us together. Neither of us would be free until I released myself inside of her.

She quickly gave up trying to escape as her body trembled violently and she let out a muffled scream as she buried her face against me again.

My viln erupted inside of her, pulsing in her depths as it released everything it contained inside of her. Each sensation sent a wave of electricity and coolness across my body as she shuddered and gasped.

I wrapped my free hand around her, holding her tightly as we both ascended to ecstasy.

CHAPTER TEN

ABIGAIL

Taren had broken something inside of me, but in a good way. I had never had an orgasm that intensely before. No one had ever worked hard enough to get me there. I giggled to myself in the mirror as I washed the sweat from my face. I can't believe I tried to stop it. It had just felt like too much. As freaky as it was, I'm grateful for whatever that stone thing holding us together was.

My body was still hot and felt sensitive. It was craving more of him, more of his heat, more of his cock. It moving on its own was another thing that was a little freaky, but hot damn it knew what it was doing.

Plus, the heat radiating off of it was intense. I don't know if that increased my blood flow or something, but I'd never felt anything like that.

A knock sounded from the door to the bathroom and I felt a grin slip up my face again. "Yes?"

"See. I am knocking before I enter. If you are pleasuring yourself, let me know and I will not enter."

I giggled. "If I was pleasuring myself, I'd want you to come help."

The door slid open, revealing Taren completely nude. I gaped a little. His body truly was immaculate, red skin or not, and it made me feel even warmer than I already was. I felt worn out, but I could still go for another round. I think.

"Should have taken that shirt off when we were having sex. Mmm," I said, looking him up and down. Taren had instilled a strange confidence in me I normally didn't have. It felt right with him. Like I could actually be myself and not have to pretend, or be some quiet servant.

"I regret it too," he said. "I would have liked to feel you against my skin." His cock twitched between his legs. *Guess he's picturing it.*

I was picturing it too. Then again, I would have probably melted from the heat. I already felt a little gross for how much I had sweated, but he was really hot. Not attractive hot, but actually hot temperature-wise. Attractive hot too, though.

"I'm going to have a shower." I looked Taren over and winked. "You can join me."

"I would like that very much," he said, slip-

ping past me. His cock reached out of its own accord and grazed my naked thigh, leaving a faint
trace of heat behind.

Taren tapped a console by the shower a
few times and it exploded into a gushing water-
fall inside the chamber. The walls quickly fogged
up with steam and the temperature in the room
increased rapidly, heat seeping through the closed
door of the shower.

My eyes went wide at the insane amount
of steam billowing through the shower door and I
made a thoughtful noise, unconsciously stepping
back. Taren glanced back at me and then to the
shower again.

"Ah. That's probably too hot for you. What's
a pleasant temperature for you?" Taren asked,
hand hovering over the console.

"What's it even on now?"

"Six hundred and twenty-seven degrees."

"Fahrenheit, celsius?" Not that it mattered.
It looked like it would melt my skin off either way.

"What?"

"Oh... right, ummm. I don't know what
temperature you all use out here."

"It is called Vargles."

"No idea what that is."

"It ranges from zero to very hot. Even for me," Taren chuckled.

"Well... can we do like... a third of whatever you have it on?" I asked, hoping that it would be somewhere in the ballpark of a comfortable shower.

"If you want," he said, tilting his head. "I enjoy a cold shower from time to time."

Taren adjusted the temperature, and the steam dissipated drastically, but still left a healthy amount. He opened the door and stuck his hand in, shuddering as he pulled it out. A smile flashed across his face and he said, "I will need a moment."

I joined him at the door, caressing his chest gently and placing my other hand into the water. It felt perfect to me. Nice and hot, but not skin-melting hot.

"This is hot to me," I said, patting him on the chest with my wet hand. "How are you not freezing standing in the room if you think this is cold? It's like seventy degrees in here. The shower has to be a hundred at least." My brain flashed some information about Luranins at me before Taren responded, and I added, "Never mind, I actually know that." I giggled and kissed him on the chest.

Luranins can regulate their body temperature and keep them comfortable no matter how hot or cold it is, but being doused or submerged in liquid disrupts that. It's apparently the only way to make them cold.

It felt odd knowing things I didn't fully understand. All of these equations were in my head, explaining how their bodies regulated themselves, but I didn't understand a lick of it.

I winked at Taren again and sidled into the shower, beckoning him behind me, focusing on swaying my hips as suggestively as possible. A little too focused. Because of the steam, I hadn't noticed all the jets of water in the shower. They were coming out of the walls, ceiling, and floor. I would have been thrilled if I hadn't immediately been blasted in the face by a jet of water coming out of the wall.

It hit me square in the eyes and I stumbled, stepping on a jet coming out of the floor, which startled me and caused me to backtrack. My life flashed before my eyes as my feet slid out from under me and I fell backward toward the glass wall.

Heat enveloped me as my body collided with Taren's, his thick arms wrapping around me tightly and his cock taking full advantage of the proximity and rubbing up and down against my ass cheek.

"I thought I was going to die." I fell into a fit of giggles as Taren helped me to my feet. He shivered against me, but seemed mostly okay. "Thanks." I puckered my lips at him, but left my eyes open to make sure he responded correctly this time.

His lips met mine, and I felt his tongue dip into my mouth, sending a pang of arousal through my body that rippled through me and into my core.

I pulled away from him and giggled again. "Thank you kisses don't involve tongue," I teased him, wagging my finger in front of him.

"Which kind do involve tongue?" he asked, pressing himself behind me. I felt his thick cock brushing against me, begging for attention.

"The fun ones," I replied, leaning against him and reaching behind me to rub his thighs. With a little stretching, I even managed to dip behind him and give his firm ass a little squeeze.

Taren's heat paired with the hot shower was making my blood flow in all the best ways, and I felt myself getting worked up as a familiar aching throb radiated from between my legs. I had been halfway there this whole time, but feeling his hard body against mine pushed me to be all the way there.

Breaking free of his grasp, I spun around

and stole a glance down his body, resisting the urge to grab his cock and put him inside of me. I wanted it, but I wanted a little fun beforehand too.

I had never had a lover be so considerate of me, and take their time with me. My experience was minimal, granted, but it had always focused on the guy getting off and never on me. I thought that was just how it was, but now... Now I see it doesn't have to be only that way.

I sighed heavily and shook my head, thoughts of my life on Earth dampening my spirits.

"What's wrong?" Taren asked gently, moving closer to me and pulling me into his arms. His cock behaved itself... a little. It still caressed me occasionally, but had quit being as persistent.

"Earth sucks."

"I do not understand. The gravity?"

"No," I giggled and pressed my face against his chest as he rubbed my back. "It's not fun."

"It seemed pleasant enough."

"I guess it can be. I didn't get to experience a lot of it."

"Why not?"

"I don't want to talk about it." It pained me thinking about all the time I wasted being controlled and not allowed to do anything.

I laughed maniacally against Taren's chest, which I'm sure confused him. It was just funny to me I was so torn up about Jason leaving me, but it ended up being the best thing possible. Taren had shown me that all men weren't like that. I wasn't useless. I wasn't just a servant and there to do as I was told.

"Do you need to rest?" Taren asked, continuing to stroke my back with both his hands.

"No," I said, pulling away from him and looking around the shower. It was time to forget. I wasn't even on the same planet anymore. Fuck Jason, fuck my old life. I'm Space Pirate Abigail now. "Damn straight," I muttered as I walked through the large shower, searching for soap.

"What are you doing?" Taren asked, watching me intently as I scoured the massive space.

"Looking for soap."

The second the word soap left my mouth, a nozzle descended from the ceiling with a small console on it. It was labeled 'cleaning products,' which made me think of things like bleach and chemicals. Those were on the list of available choices, but it also had normal soap with various fragrances.

Even with the translator, all the scents were

gibberish to me. Except for banana, oddly.

"Come pick a soap," I said. Taren approached me slowly, stopping just short of touching me and looking over my shoulder. I leaned back into him and returned to stroking his thighs. His cock perked up instantly, planting itself against my body and rubbing itself across my lower back.

Taren tapped through the list, reaching over me, and chose a smell called Flugneld. The nozzle on the dispenser lit up, and I put my hand under it. It spurted out a lime-green goo that, when paired with the name Flugneld, grossed me out for a second.

Until the scent hit me. A little like green apple and pine, the smell that Taren always had wafting off him. I took a deep whiff of the soap and turned around to face Taren.

My hands slid with ease across each dip and groove in his hard body as I rubbed the slippery soap across his shoulders and down his arms. The second I touched him with the soap, the water pouring onto us disappeared, leaving us in a dry circle amidst a torrent of water.

"I can bathe myself," Taren said with a smirk, but let out a satisfied grunt when I pressed against him to run my soapy hands across his back. His skin rippled under my touch, the rough stone texture tickling the palm of my hand as it passed. It had weirded me out when it happened earlier, but it was a pleasant sensation, and thankfully his cock hadn't done that while he was inside of me.

The heat between my hands as I gripped his thick bicep and ran them down to his wrist sent a tremor through me. The slipperiness and the heat made my mind wander.

Images of his cock sliding into my dripping folds filled my brain as I absently took his hand in both of mine, squeezing and rubbing his fingers suggestively.

"I believe that is clean."

"Mhmm," I replied, pushing against him again after getting another handful of soap. My fingers slid across his lower back, his ass cheeks, down the back of his thighs. I slowly got to my knees, his cock right in my face, as I continued to lather him up.

It was begging for its turn. I could feel it, but it would have to wait 'til I was done. For once in my life, I was in control, and I was going to take my time. *It'll pay off, I promise, big guy.*

My own body was already past the breaking point and all but begging me to do something besides rub on him. It was ready for its turn to be rubbed on. To be massaged. To be penetrated.

I closed my eyes and bit my lip as I tried to calm myself. It didn't work, and I gripped his cock with a soapy hand. My body got hotter as I continued stroking its shaft slowly and relishing the feeling of the thick, hot flesh between my fingers. It stopped moving and became straight and rigid, letting me run my hand across its full length without issue as I put my mouth around the girthy head, careful to stop before I hit the part with soap.

Ridges prickled up across his length. The soap let my fingers slip across them with ease, adding an almost vibrating sensation to each movement I made.

Taren groaned above me, and the sound pushed my clit into overdrive, the aching throb too much to resist. I took my other hand off his thigh and dove it between my own legs, lightly sliding my finger across the swollen nub.

A gentle tap was all it took to send an electric shiver through my body and I moaned against the cock in my mouth, prompting Taren to groan again as I ran my finger across my clit.

I felt Taren's hands slip under my arms, but I didn't fully register what was happening as his cock slid out of my mouth and I found myself on my feet again. Briefly.

They left the ground a moment later, and I was slammed against a wall as the sheet of water cleared a path for us.

Taren's cock wormed its way between my legs and dove into my folds with gusto. Each ridge sent a tingle through my body as it passed my lips and slipped into my depths. I shuddered as it twisted inside of me and retreated to the very edge before diving back inside and twisting. *That's new.* I tried to say something, but the only thing that came out was, "Oh, oh, that's so good." It was close enough to what I wanted to say, at least.

A single glance at Taren's vibrant purple eyes was all it took to push me over the edge. I let out a long moan that was met with a tight grip around my waist as the stoney protrusion enveloped me again.

Taren's cock continued to move inside of me, unhindered by our bodies being locked together. His hands squeezed my ass tightly as I planted my face on his chest and closed my eyes tightly, riding the intense electric wave as I came.

The wave swelled to new heights when his cock grew thicker inside me and pulsed in my depths. Filling me to the brim with heat as Taren squeezed me tighter and buried his face in the top of my head.

I thought I was going to black out from all the overwhelming sensations, but I successfully stayed awake. Taren sat me down gently as the stone released me and I wobbled slightly in his arms before saying, "I'm good, I'm good."

Our fingers interlocked as I took his hand and pulled him back to the center of the shower.

"Okay, we need to actually bathe now," I said, my body soaking wet with sweat from the heat of his body. "I'm all gross and sweaty."

"You are not gross," Taren said from behind me. "I find your scent intoxicating, especially after you perspired."

"That's… kinda gross too," I giggled. "But I appreciate it." I really did. It was nice knowing someone liked every aspect of me.

Taren stood above me, closing his eyes and puckering his lips out. He smacked them loudly, as if he was asking for a kiss from me. From two feet above my head.

"Seriously?"

"I always bend down to kiss you. It's only fair that you come to me sometimes," he replied, not opening his eyes and continuing to smack his lips.

"If only I could grow two feet."

"You have two feet."

"Shut the fuck up, Taren." I burst into laughter and grabbed his neck, pulling him down to my level and planting a wet kiss on his lips.

CHAPTER ELEVEN
ABIGAIL

"We need to return to the ship," Taren said from under me. I closed my eyes and listened to his heart thud away in his chest, relishing the heat pouring off of him and into my cheek.

"If we have to," I whispered, planting a kiss on his bare skin and giggling as a ripple of stone washed across his body.

"We do not have to do anything."

"But we should, right?"

Taren sighed. "Yes. Deborah should not do the transaction alone."

"You don't trust her?"

Taren sat up quickly and dumped my head into his lap. I could feel his cock pressing against my face under the thick blanket, begging me to grab it. My hand dipped under the covers and ran across his thigh, lightly grazing his shaft with a fingertip, but I retrieved it quickly and let out a sigh. My body wasn't ready for another go just yet. He was a shockingly considerate lover, but he still wore me out and made me feel weak.

"I trust her, but she should not go alone. The people we are dealing with are not the most trustworthy," Taren said, running his fingers through my hair.

"Well, we better offer her some backup then," I said, leaping to my feet and offering Taren a hand.

He took my hand and pulled me back onto his lap. We giggled, teasing, and batting at the other playfully for several seconds before Taren fell silent and looked at me with his purple eyes. "You should stay here."

"What? No. Why?"

"It's dangerous."

"I don't care. I'm going with you two. Besides, both of you can protect me if something happens. Right?" I poked him in his firm chest as he stared at me. "Right?"

"Yes, we can."

"Then there's no problem!" I hopped out of bed again and offered him my hand. He reached for it and I pulled it away before he could grab it, giggling and rushing to get dressed.

"Real cute," he muttered, climbing out of bed and throwing his clothes on.

"I do my best," I replied. Watching him squeeze that delicious booty into his tight pants. It's a shame that we have to cut our little vacation short. *Plenty of time on the ship, though.*

"So, what's the plan for me?" I asked as we boarded the grav-lift. This one, thankfully, had a solid floor.

"What do you mean?" Taren asked.

"Are you taking me back to Earth?"

His face fell flat. "If you wish."

"I mean, not really. It'd be hard to return there knowing all of this was out here. I didn't have a lot going on anyway."

"I can take you anywhere you want."

"I think I'd like to just stay with you and Deborah. If that's okay." It seemed crazy to not want to return to Earth, but I really didn't want to go back. There was so much to see out in the universe, and going back to my boring job and lonely life seemed like the worst idea. I could stay on QT-314, but then what? Get another job in a store? Sure, I'd get to see crazy aliens and technology, but in the end, it wouldn't be much different. Might as well become a smuggler or whatever.

Most importantly, I didn't want to leave Taren.

Taren appeared deep in thought, dramatically stroking his chin as he made a thoughtful noise. "I suppose that is fine, for the time being."

"For the time being?"

He smirked. "For as long as you want."

Taren snagged the last vulru roll from the tray that room service had left us earlier. He had ordered us an obscene amount of food, and I couldn't even taste most of it before getting full. Taren apparently had no issues with getting full, as he had devoured the majority of it. I picked up my glass of baktoo and finished it, setting it on a table by the door as we left.

"What is that even?" I asked, looking at the shimmering vulru roll in his hand as we walked toward the grav-lift.

He chewed thoughtfully, swallowing when we stepped onto the grav-lift and replied, "A vulru roll."

"I know... you told me that already. What's in it?"

"Vulru."

"You are maddening sometimes."

He offered the roll to me, half of it already

gone. It looked like a burrito, the exterior white with brown spots, but the stuffing was a green goo with every color of the rainbow present in chunks suspended inside the goo.

I winced as he moved it closer and closer to my face, a bizarre smell that was like a mix of coconut, parmesan, and eggs assaulting my nose.

"You know what? Never mind, I don't want to know," I said, holding up my hand.

"Your loss." Taren crammed the rest of the roll into his mouth.

The door to the grav-lift opened and Taren froze immediately as we stepped off, taking my hand and pulling me against the wall at the top of the stairs. We crouched down behind a fluffy purple plant and he peered through its leaves.

"What's wrong?" I whispered.

"The people hunting me on Earth are here. The Purveyors," he whispered, motioning towards half a dozen people in heavy coats and armor, faces completely covered except for their eyes. They were surrounding the Treglonical.

"What do we do?" I asked, my eyes going wide as Taren pulled out a small gun and placed a tiny orb inside of it.

"We improvise."

"What's that?"

"You will see," he said, aiming the gun at the Treglonical. It fired with a quiet 'fwompf' and the tiny orb looked like a blur as it flew through the air. It missed the little rat creature and hit just under the desk in front of the people in coats.

Taren turned a dial on the gun, and the side opened up as he stared at the group. I started to ask what he was doing, but the Treglonical turned its back to the others and dug through a cabinet for something.

"Stupid little Treglonical knows nothing," Taren whispered into the side of the gun. The little rat person froze, staring across the lobby as its body twitched.

"Shush, what are you doing?" a voice played back from his gun.

"I did not say anything."

"Who said that?"

"Keep quiet."

"Treglonicals are nothing but blysh. We should just kill it and move on," Taren whispered into the gun. "Hey, Treglonical, hurry up."

"Who the fuck is saying that?"

The Treglonical turned around and faced the group of people. It was already triple its normal size and the small jumpsuit it was wearing was straining to hold itself together as its muscles bulged.

Its snout stretched to an unnatural length and long fangs grew from its jaw. The claws at the end of its hands were already half a foot long and thickening as it stared at the men in coats.

"What are you looking at, Treglonical?" Taren whispered into the gun.

That was all the final straw. The now massive and hulking rat person leapt over the desk, cleaving parts off the men in coats and tossing their bodies across the lobby.

Taren tucked his gun into his coat and took my hand. "Stay close."

We rushed down the stairs and past the chaos the Treglonical was causing as it tore the men limb from limb, splattering blood and body parts, tarnishing the pristine lobby. A bar on the far wall had a small blue man behind it, peeking out from under a blast-shield as it slowly closed over the bar. *Guess this isn't the first time this has happened.*

I tried not to look as we rushed past. I didn't want to see the evisceration that the Treglonical was currently in the middle of, and I also didn't want to accidentally make eye contact and anger it.

We burst through the door of the hotel just as a loud splatter sounded behind us. Both of us glanced back to see the glass door covered in dripping blood before we toppled over as we ran into a set of blue Doldos.

Taren pulled me tight as we fell down the stairs, his body shifting to stone against me. He landed with a loud crash and quickly stood up, lifting me with him and setting me on my feet.

"Are you okay?" he asked, smoothing out my cloak.

"Yeah, I'm fine. That was insane," I replied shakily. My heart was beating frantically and my breath was shallow, but at least we weren't hurt.

"All in a day's work," he said with a grin. "I would not go in there for a while," he added, talking to the Doldos. They both looked from him to the blood dripping down the doorway before shrugging and stepping into the hotel.

"Why the hell would they go in there?" I asked, glimpsing the still rampaging Treglonical before the door closed again. It was slamming one Purveyor repeatedly into the ground.

"Probably something they have seen before." Taren shrugged. "Come on." He took me under his arm and we started our journey to the landing bay.

CHAPTER TWELVE
ABIGAIL

Deborah was already at the ship and waiting impatiently, tapping her foot far too loudly as we approached.

"It is about time," she huffed, marching up the ramp of the ship and returning with a floating cart that had the sealed crates stacked onto it. "Why can you never be on time?"

"We ran into…" Taren started.

"Trouble. There is always trouble, Taren. You should know that by now and account for it in your calculations for your arrival at a designated meeting point at a specific time."

"How am I supposed to account for that? I never know what will happen."

"I was attacked by a Mikra in the light-wind on the way here and I arrived on time," Deborah stated as she placed a dark tarp over the crates.

"That does not… a Mikra, seriously?"

"Yes. You are always in a rush, never stopping to think and observe."

I had noticed that about Taren; he was constantly doing something and on the move. He really needed to settle down and smell the roses.

I was honestly a little surprised that he spent so much time with me in the hotel room with how quickly he moved through the station before.

"She's right, you know," I added. "You should slow down sometimes. It's not healthy to constantly be rushing about. You have to clear your head and relax sometimes."

"Both of you, go ahead, pile on," Taren chuckled.

He was always unphased too. That was something I wish would rub off on me. I only pretend to be unphased. I've honestly had this underlying sense of terror buried inside of me since the grocery store.

Hopefully, I had it under control, but I was worried it would pop up at any time. With Taren and Deborah around, I probably didn't have to worry.

"We are both correct in our observations," Deborah stated, before turning to me. "You should have coerced him into leaving sooner."

"Sorry, Deborah," I offered. I wasn't sure how anyone could actually coerce Taren, but I guess I could have tried.

"Thank you, that is all I wanted," she replied cheerfully. "The meeting is in the usual location, so we will have an hour of walking. *I* accounted for your tardiness. We have two hours to get there."

"You're the best," I said with a grin.

"I am well aware and not informed of that enough," Deborah quipped.

"Thank you Deborah," Taren said, extending his hand to her. She tilted her head and let out a quiet sigh before slapping his hand with hers like a sideways high five.

"What are we doing after the meeting?" I asked as we moved back into the station.

"Whatever we want, there will be plenty of credits to go around," Taren said happily.

"Are we going to leave the station?"

"We can stay for a while. I have no issue with it and I am sure Deborah will be getting some upgrades."

"Already picked them out," Deborah replied with a smile in her voice.

I looked up at the giant red man to my left

and the jet-black blank-faced bionic woman to my right and sighed pensively.

It was hard to believe that in such a short amount of time my life had changed so dramatically. I would have never dreamed I would end up anywhere like this, let alone with a robot and an alien. My bizarre new family. It was perfect.

My knees went weak, and I leaned against Taren as I looked down and saw that we were on the glass-floored lift high above the city street.

I hadn't even been paying attention to where we were walking and just followed them blindly onto it. *I really need to watch where I'm walking.*

That would be wise.

Taren's arm found itself around me and he held me tightly as the lift dropped us to the street. It was easier this time, but still did a number on my stomach, and I moved a little slowly for a few minutes after getting off. Taren and Deborah slowed their pace until I steadied myself and walked normally again.

"Are we walking or taking the light-wind?" I asked as we passed one of the turquoise cylinders.

"The light-wind is dangerous even when you are not transporting cargo," Deborah said. "We are walking."

Deborah shifted to the back of the cart while me and Taren stood side by side at the front as we escorted our cargo through the busy street.

Weaving through the massive crowds in the district, each of us remained silent and focused on maneuvering through the thick walls of flesh, metal, and who-knows-what that the myriad of aliens were made of. It was way more crowded than the last time we were here and I wondered if it was some special occasion. *Maybe it's the weekend.*

A visible line was in the road. Not a painted one, but a line that showed where the people that cleaned and repaired the station stopped.

The streets, sidewalks, and buildings instantly became dilapidated and in need of serious maintenance when we crossed and the crowds thinned out significantly as we passed a sign marking the entrance to the Nythyx district.

"This place looks incredibly sketchy," I mumbled, my head on a swivel as he pressed forward.

"It is. Stick close," Taren whispered, stepping closer to me. His hand dipped into his coat, no doubt holding onto a weapon. I mirrored him and tucked my hand under my cloak, holding the grip of my gun tightly.

Most of the shops had heavy metal grating over their windows, offering only a tiny view of what was inside. The few people in the streets were in groups of three or more and sticking together tightly as they looked around nervously.

A few of the shops had massive aliens leaning against the walls by the doors, each a different species, and each larger than the last. They were all armed to the teeth with a wide variety of weapons, swords, guns, axes, long circular blades.

"Guards," Taren murmured as we passed one shop. "For the shops that can afford their protection."

"Is it like a mafia thing?"

"A what?"

"It'd be a shame if something happened to your store. Pay us and we'll make sure nothing does," I said with my best accent.

"Yes," Deborah chimed in from behind.

One alien bellowed loudly as we passed, like a cow excited about its dinner. I jumped and turned to face it, my heart racing and almost pulling out my gun.

It was staring directly at me with its huge black eyes set behind a sharp blue nose. It grinned, revealing hundreds of sharpened teeth as its shoulders heaved up and down in a fit of laughter.

"Hilarious," I muttered, stepping even closer to Taren.

After another twenty minutes of walking, Taren glanced into one of the barricaded shop windows and did a double take, stopping suddenly. Deborah slammed the cart into the back of his knees, and he almost toppled over.

"Watch it," he said, bending down to rub the back of his leg.

"You should not have stopped suddenly," Deborah remarked.

"What are you doing?" I asked as Taren slipped around me and stepped onto the sidewalk, pressing his face against the metal grid across the window.

"You two go on ahead. I'll catch up," Taren said, dipping into an alley beside the store.

The back of the cart nudged me gently, and I started walking, staring down the alley as we passed to see Taren hunched down in front of a door.

"What's he doing?" I asked, looking back at Deborah.

"I do not know. Keep your eyes forward, please. Do not let your guard down."

The nervousness that had been brewing

just below the surface welled to the top and threatened to flood my brain now that Taren was gone.
I tried to keep reassuring myself that Deborah was
here and I would be okay, but she seemed so far
away from me, even though it was just a few feet.

We continued on, the random guards in
front of shops leering at us as we passed, no doubt
debating on whether or not to take whatever we
were carting. Two small women were a much easier target than Taren.

Hopefully they could tell Deborah wasn't
one to be trifled with. I could put up a fight, too,
I had no doubt about that. I just wasn't sure how
much of a fight, and I didn't really want to find out.

Are there like… training neurlin-relogs?

What do you mean?

Like for combat?

Yes. They are not as effective as actual training
since they do not provide the muscle memory, but
they will teach you tactics and theories.

I made a thoughtful noise and glanced
around again, anxious for Taren to reappear. It had
been at least ten minutes and I was starting to
worry.

"Run," Deborah said suddenly. I didn't need
her to tell me twice and sprinted ahead immediately, glancing over my shoulder to find Deborah

and the cart directly behind me. "Right."

We ducked into an alley, startling two smaller aliens in the middle of some kind of transaction. All of their eyes went wide, and they scurried off deeper into the alley, exchanging curses with one another.

The cart fell to the ground with a thump and Deborah grabbed my arm, pulling me down behind it. We both peered over the tarp-covered crates and waited for whatever was coming.

"What's happening?" I whispered.

Taren is coming and told us to run and hide.

"Why?" I was getting incredibly nervous and drew my gun.

"Stay here," Deborah replied, slipping from behind the crates before I could respond and moving to the end of the alley.

Thumping footsteps grew louder and louder as she leaned forward and raised her hands.

"What the…" Taren said, his body a blur as Deborah snatched him from the street and pulled him behind the crates with me. "Thanks."

A few seconds later, more thumping footsteps approached, half a dozen of the alien guards rushing past the alley in hot pursuit of someone. Taren, I'd bet.

Taren chuckled quietly and turned around, leaning against the stack of crates as he pulled a long, slender gun from his coat. He looked over and pulled a couple of levers on it. The gun clicked quietly before releasing a hiss of blue steam.

"Still in good condition." He nodded at the gun and tucked it into his coat before lifting a small dingy silver bracelet set with black and red gemstone out.

A smile crept up his face before he caught me staring and quickly pushed it back into his coat.

"Please, someone tell me what's going on," I demanded.

"I stole my gun back," Taren said off-handedly. "Let's go."

"Aren't they looking for you? How are we going to go anywhere?"

"No, they did not see me. They just knew someone stole it," he chuckled. "We will come up behind them. It's fine. Probably."

"Probably?"

"Yep, probably."

Deborah did not say a word and reactivated the cart. It hovered in the air slowly and she motioned for us to get in the front. I had so many more questions, but kept them to myself and joined Taren at the front of the cart as we moved back into the street.

"Did you obtain something else?" Deborah asked, clearly knowing something I didn't.

"Yes," Taren replied, glancing over his shoulder. "No more questions."

"Very well."

As much as I liked the two of them, they could be infuriating, and I knew if I pressed for an-swers, I would get nothing but frustration.

The group of guards that were chasing Taren disappeared around a corner ahead and we marched forward. Another divide was coming up, hopefully to a safer district.

It had felt like I was being watched from the moment we stepped into this district, and I was anxious to be out of it. Especially now that Taren was being hunted for stealing a gun.

I wanted to chastise him for doing that right now. It seemed like something that could have at least waited until we weren't carting a for-tune's worth of bananas. The more I thought about it, the more irritated I got with the unnecessary theft, but I kept silent and walked beside him.

He seemed happy with himself, and I didn't want to spoil the mood. Besides, nothing bad came from it... yet, at least.

The next district grew closer and closer. It looked much cleaner than the one we were currently in and the border had several station guards posted around it in their pristine white armor, each of them careful not to step across the line.

They all watched us as we approached, analyzing our movements, hands on their weapons, ready for whatever trouble we may bring.

The group chasing Taren earlier reappeared from an alley, and I held my breath as they passed us, murmuring about how they lost whoever they were chasing. All six of them didn't give us a second glance and when we were clear, I let out my breath and shot Taren a dirty glare.

"I told you it was fine," he whispered with a smirk. I couldn't help but smile back at him, even though I was frustrated with the stress he just put me through.

"Well, well," a gravelly voice said from the last alley before the new district. We were so close, but not close enough, and my heart sank as four Purveyors stepped into the street with their weapons raised. "Had a suspicion you'd be coming through this way."

"Stand aside," Taren said calmly. "We do not want any trouble."

"You killed the others, had them torn to shreds, and you say you do not want trouble?" one of the other Purveyors said snidely.

"They got themselves killed. They should have known better than to insult a," Taren said, pausing to glance around. "Treglonical."

"I have word that you instigated that reaction," the first Purveyor said. "Tell you what. Give us the crates. We'll cut off a hand. Then we can go our separate ways."

"Sounds like a fair deal," Taren said with a grin, glancing at me and back at Deborah. "Come over here and take them." Taren placed his wrist on the top of a crate and pulled back his sleeve. "Take this one. I need the other."

"He uses his right hand to…" Deborah started, but Taren glared at her and she fell silent.

The Purveyor's eyed him suspiciously as they approached, weapons raised and at the ready. The station guards watched with interest from the line, but made no move to help us.

Taren had told me before they didn't dare to cross some of the district lines, and that was probably one of them.

A muffled whir sounded from behind me, and I stole a peek at Deborah. The sound was definitely coming from her, but she was statuesque and gave no indication of what she was doing.

My hand subconsciously dipped under my cloak and I gripped the handle of my gun, praying to whoever would listen that I'd know what to do when the time came.

The four Purveyors stopped a few feet away. Taren and Deborah had still not moved, but something had changed.

All four of the Purveyors turned their gaze to me, and the first one said, "Your mate, huh? I can smell it in the air. She marked you." Their weapons all fell onto me as they shuffled to my side of the cart and stepped closer. *I marked him?*

The faint smile on Taren's face faded and turned into a scowl that grew harsher with each step they took toward me.

He moved his arm from the crate, but the Purveyor shouted, "No, no. You move and we'll fill her so full of plasma you'll have nothing left to fuck."

Taren's hand thudded loudly as it fell back onto the crate. I met his eyes as they flickered to that deep crimson red, and I braced myself for whatever was about to happen.

"That's right, you have no choice but to protect her," the Purveyor said, slipping up behind me and placing his gun to my head as he pulled me tightly against his body. He sniffed loudly before continuing, "Oh, she's a fine one, too. Now you just sit there all pretty while we slice off that hand of yours and take these bananas."

The gun against my head clicked loudly and I could see a faint green glow from the corner of my eye.

They apparently didn't view me as a threat, not even making me show my hands. I kept a tight grip on the handle of my gun and waited for Taren or Deborah to make a move.

You may get injured.

Whatever we have to do, Deborah.

When you hear a bell ring, drop to the ground immediately.

What are they talking about, me marking Taren?

It is not relevant at the moment. Focus.

The Purveyor holding me pulled me further away from the cart and onto the sidewalk while the other three circled Taren. One of them holstered their gun and drew a long, slender blade, before glancing at the one that had me captive. I guess he was the leader.

"Yeah, go on," the gravelly voice said behind me.

The Purveyor lifted the blade without further instruction and slid it through the air with lightning speed.

A sharp clang made me grit my teeth as the blade met Taren's wrist, shattering against the stone suddenly coating Taren's arm.

A bell chimed, and I went completely limp, slipping out of the unsuspecting Purveyor's arm and collapsing to the ground as a metal disc flew out of Deborah's chest. It exploded in a burst of blinding white light as it separated into four thin discs, each of them flying towards the Purveyors.

Taren hit the ground just as the first disc collided with the neck of the woman still staring in shock at her broken blade. Her head toppled to the ground unceremoniously as the other two Purveyors beside her met a similar fate.

I don't know if the Purveyor with me was faster, or the distance bought him some extra time, but he ducked under the disc at the last second, falling to the ground beside me. I was in his arms again in a flash, lifted to my feet with a gun back against my temple.

"Real cute," the remaining Purveyor said, pulling me painfully tight against him with his arm across my neck. The barrel of his gun pressed so hard on my temple that I was worried he was going to drive it into my skull.

"Let her go," Taren demanded, vaulting across the cart and leveling his own gun with the Purveyor's head.

"Oh," the Purveyor chuckled. "You might hit her. I know how your bonds work. You can't put her in danger." He breathed in deeply, burying his face in the back of my head against the cloak. I could feel his hot breath through the fabric.

"Not until I have mated with her," Taren said, adjusting the aim of his gun to keep track of the Purveyor as he shifted around and placed his arm on my shoulder, aiming his own gun back at Taren.

I grabbed the hilt of my blade, drawing it quickly, and plunging it behind me blindly. It met resistance, and I pressed the buttons on the hilt. I could feel the intense heat emanating from the blade behind me.

It slipped through the Purveyor's armor, prompting a howl of rage from him, but his grip only tightened and he didn't release me.

The Purveyor grunted, then chuckled quietly. "It'll take more than a little heat to take me down. We're from the same planet, you know."

I twisted the blade and flailed in his grip, but he tightened his hold across my throat and I gasped for air, releasing the hilt and clawing frantically at his thick arm.

"Let me go," I wheezed, trying to dig my fingernails into his thick flesh.

"If you harm her, I will rend you limb from limb. Slowly," Taren said, his voice terrifyingly calm and his eyes darkened to blood red.

"You can threaten me all you like, but I've got all the cards right now," the Purveyor replied, but he loosened his grip on my throat.

I took in a huge gulp of air and panted against his arm. After a few seconds of fresh air, I pulled the gun out of my cloak, aimed it beside my head, and fired a blue blast behind me with a quiet 'whomp.'

The purveyor let out another screech of rage, but kept his grip on me as I fired another blast into his chest. His body convulsed, and his grip tightened even further as I shot into him again. He fell backward onto the ground, spasming violently and pulling me with him as I tried to wiggle free of his ever-tightening grip.

His arm choked me, and this time it was so tight I couldn't even draw in a tiny breath.

Thankfully, Taren had sprinted over to us before we even hit the ground, and grabbed the Purveyor's arm with both his hands, wrenching it upward with a sickening crunch as he broke the arm and freed me from his grip.

I scrambled to my feet, standing beside Taren and planting my hands on my knees as I panted wildly, trying to recover my breath.

The Purveyor's body was convulsing on the ground, blue steam seeping out of his eyes and through the bandana over his nose and mouth.

"Three shots was a little overkill," Taren said off-handedly, watching the Purveyor twitch. "But it is pleasant to see."

"What's happening?" I asked, taking one last deep breath before finding myself back to normal. "I thought that was a stun gun?"

"It's a molecular-destabilizing neuron accelerator," Taren replied matter-of-factly.

"We need to continue on," Deborah said, completely unfazed by what just happened. "We are getting low on time."

"Yeah, come on," Taren said, patting me on the shoulder. "Good job."

We returned to the cart and started moving towards the other district again. The station guards exchanged glances before fidgeting nervously and watching our approach.

"Deborah told me it was a stun gun," I said, wondering if I killed that man. Not that he didn't deserve it… probably. I still wasn't too keen on the idea of taking someone's life.

"It does stun them," Deborah said flatly.

"Then kills them," Taren added. "Very effective."

"That's not what…"

"Halt. What business do you have here?" a station guard asked, each of them raising their weapons unconfidently.

"We mean no harm. We are merely merchants looking to off-load some wares with Mishikantz."

At the mention of the name Mishikantz, the guards immediately lowered their weapons and motioned us through. One of them mumbled about having to look at those bodies all day and wondered aloud if the cleaners would cross the line a few feet to move them.

"Thanks for the help," I muttered as we walked between them. Most of them ignored me, but one of them offered an apologetic shrug.

CHAPTER THIRTEEN
TAREN

It was relieving to be out of the Nythyx district and into Mishikantz's territory. It was just as shady and full of sketchy dealings, but they at least kept it clean and relatively organized. The buildings were not uniform, but most were the same shade of green and the same general shape. Now that we were known to be meeting with Mishikantz, we should have little trouble going forward.

"What did he mean? I marked you?" Abigail asked, peering at me inquisitively.

"Have you not informed her?" Deborah chimed in. "I expressly told you to inform her."

"Inform me of what?"

"It did not seem to matter," I said. I really did not believe it mattered. We had a connection, that much was certain. Whether or not she marked me, it should not matter. I would have desired her, anyway. Hells, I desired her anyway, long before she marked me. Maybe not as fervently, but I did.

"If you do not tell her, I will. Right now," Deborah said. She sounded irritated and disappointed in me. A tone I was quite used to hearing from her.

"When you licked my hand, you marked me as your mate," I said. *Might as well get this over with.*

"What does that even mean?" Abigail asked.

"Is that not in your species compendium?"

"I don't know anything about any mating stuff."

I scoffed, "For that price, it should have had everything."

"Well, it didn't. Now tell me what the hell you two are talking about. No games."

"When your saliva comes in contact with a male Luranin's palm, it marks you as their mate."

"Okay... what does that entail?"

"Well... uncontrollable desire to protect."

"So you've just been taking care of me this whole time because you have to?"

"No. Once we mated, it wore off."

"What do you mean, it wore off?"

"I do not have a desire to protect you any-more." I could see the hurt growing in her eyes and immediately felt like I could have worded that better. The haze over my mind that kept me focused on her was still present, but I had more control over myself than before. The Call of the Vreth should release me fully soon, and I would know for sure how I felt.

Smooth.

Not now.

"I mean that I have control over it. I wish to keep you safe," I said hastily.

"Is that why you wanted to... mate with me?" There was disdain in her voice with the word 'mate.'

"Yes." More hurt in her eyes and this time I felt a pain in my central pilon. "Listen. It's biology, there's no fighting it. Yes, it made me want to mate with you and protect you." I paused, not knowing exactly where I was going with that.

"All of that was just because of biology?" Abigail asked, her voice flat and emotionless. "I thought we had something special, but it was just because I licked your hand being immature?"

We shuffled quietly down the street for a few minutes. Abigail refused to look at me, and Deborah remained awkwardly silent.

Help me out.

This is your issue to deal with. I told you to do this earlier.

"There's more to it than that," I said hesitantly. Was there more to it than that? I had never desired a mate, and I always thought of myself as being alone forever. I was happy with that. Was that really what I wanted?

Sure, I had found myself attracted to Abigail from the first time I laid eyes on her in that grocery store, but that was just an appreciation of physical beauty. Maybe. It might have been something more. Maybe I did know deep down that she was perfect for me.

Something was undoubtedly different inside of me, but I had never experienced it before, and did not know what it was exactly.

A fog had descended on my brain when the Call of the Vreth took hold and I had not felt completely clear since then. I know that I felt cool inside, happy, and comfortable. Almost like I was whole when she was around.

Luranins were not supposed to feel that way. Our women were powerful warriors that took what they wanted and then left.

There were no deeper connections, usually. I had heard stories of Vreth-lock, where two are joined for life, but it was either a myth or exceedingly rare.

Using words to express my emotions was never my strongest ability. I always just assumed people knew I cared about them. The few people I cared about, anyway. *Deborah knows I care about her. I do not have to express it directly. Right?*

It would be nice.

Thanks for finally giving input.

I sighed heavily and trudged forward. If I cannot even admit how I feel aloud, perhaps it's just the Call of the Vreth, nothing more.

No, it's more than that. It has to be. *Please let it be more than that.*

"Well?" Abigail side-eyed me, her expression unreadable.

"Well, what?"

"You said there's more to it than that. What else is there to it?"

"I do not know," I said, searching for the words to express what I felt. As much as I wanted to deny having deeper feelings for someone, they were there. My central pilon made it all too clear that I longed for Abigail in other ways, not just physical like the call demands.

"Well, that's just lovely," Abigail huffed.

ABIGAIL

The feelings I had developed for Taren were strong and fiery. That just made it hurt all the more, knowing that he couldn't help himself and was just with me because I licked his hand. *Ridiculous.* Maybe I was the one being ridiculous. I'm just some human from a backwoods planet. What chance do I have with someone like Taren?

I sighed wistfully, side-eyeing Taren and wishing desperately that he'd say something. He kept his eyes forward as we marched ahead in silence. I wanted to speak, but I couldn't even think of what to say. I didn't even know what I needed to hear right then.

Are you well?

I'm fine.

It is quite the feat to express pensivity through a neural-connection, let alone in so few words.

Thanks?

You are stronger than you think. Do not let yourself be saddened.

It's just… I thought things were different be-tween us. Is it? Do you know if he actually does care for me?

> I do not. Taren has never expressed more than a temporary interest in others. He appears to care about you, but whether that is deeper than is typ-ical, I am unsure. I do not know the markers of him caring for others beyond a superficial level. I apologize.

It's fine. Thanks anyway. Talk to you later. I don't know why I thought that last part. Some-times it felt like I was on a phone call more than a telepathic link. Deborah remained silent, appar-ently taking that as a hint to leave me alone, which made me feel guilty on top of the sadness and irri-tation I was already feeling.

"How much farther do we have to go?" I asked, finally breaking the long silence. The last district was stressful to be in, and I was a little re-lieved being in this one. It was much cleaner and organized, but something still felt off, even with the station guards scattered about.

"Mishikantz's office is just ahead," Deborah replied.

"Is there anything I should know?" My nerves were getting to me the deeper we got into the district.

"I would suggest remaining silent and not

making eye contact with anyone," Deborah said.

"Are they that bad?"

"Mishikantz is one of the foulest people in the station. They are also one of the wealthiest," Taren said quietly, glancing around at the guards. "They have free rein here, and will do as they please with no consequences."

"Keep quiet and keep my hood low, got it," I said nervously. I was deeply regretting not remaining in the hotel room.

The complications with Taren mixed with the anxiety from our upcoming meeting and made me sick to my stomach. I placed a hand across it and walked along quietly, trying to will myself to feel better.

We paused in front of an intricately decorated building. It was the same uniform color as the rest, but there were engravings etched across the entire thing. Each one had the same bizarre alien in dozens of different scenes.

Battles, victories, celebrations. All with heroic-looking poses from the incredibly buff alien. The amount of muscles on the alien put Taren's formidable body to shame.

"Is that Mishikantz?" I asked, staring at the engravings while we walked up the stairs, the cart hovering behind us as Deborah pushed from behind.

Taren chuckled quietly. "Yeah."

I didn't have time to ask why he was laughing. The door in front of us flew open and a tall, slender figure emerged. They were wrapped in white fabric from head to toe, without a sliver of skin showing. A stoney mask was set on its face and it spread its tentacle arms out in greeting.

"Welcome. You must be Taren," it said in a melodic, androgenous voice.

"You have seen me seven times, Dulren," Taren replied.

"Have I now? Well, come along. Wait," Dulren said, pausing and turning around. "We were informed you would be accompanied by a bionic only. Who is this?"

"Abigail. A new crew member," Taren said quickly.

"Species?"

"Rondal."

"Mhmm. Come along," Dulren said after staring at me for a moment, spinning around and gliding inside the massive building.

Dulren's exothandric nervous system activated.

What?

It is suspicious and on guard.

Great.

It is not.

I moved closer to Taren, resisting the urge to tuck my hands in my cloak and hold on to a weapon. There were half a dozen guards inside the sprawling white foyer, spread evenly along the walls, and it would have probably been a bad idea to make any strange movements.

Each of them stared at us intently as we passed through. I kept waiting for us to go through a metal detector or something, but we entered freely, passing through another door at the back of the room.

This room was even larger and lined with expensive looking things on shelves, tables, and pedestals. Most of it was completely foreign to me and looked straight out of a mad scientist's fever dream.

The white floors, ceiling, and walls were interrupted by thick black pillars that stretched to the ceiling far above our heads, each one wrapped in the same ornate gold filigrees as the walls.

At the center of the room was a huge u-shaped desk that looked like it was carved out of a solid piece of marble and taller than I was.

Sat behind it was the face of the alien in all the engravings on the outside of the building. The body, however, was nothing like the muscular hero outside. It was lumpy, wide, and jiggled as they turned their head to us.

It looked like it was just wearing a bedsheet with holes cut into it for its head and flAbigail pale arms to poke out of. Its beady eyes raised from a tablet on the desk and looked at us.

My head spun, trying to keep track as the dozen eyes moved independently, zipping around wildly as it looked us over.

"Ah, Taren," a sticky voice said, smacking sounds spread between each syllable. "Deborah. Who is this new one?"

"Greetings, Mishikantz. This is a new crew member. No one of consequence," Taren said calmly, moving in front of me. I peeked around him at the pile of fat behind the desk, watching its movements with a mixture of curiosity and disgust.

I was vaguely insulted by Taren saying I was no one of consequence, but I knew he was just protecting me.

"Her build is strange. What species is she?"

I shuddered as Mishikantz pulsated behind the desk and a pungent aroma that smelled similar to rotting meat wafted into my nose.

"A Rondal."

A snorting sound echoed through the room as Mishikantz's body quivered. "She does not smell like a Rondal."

"She's been traveling. It is not relevant. I have the bananas," Taren said quickly, motioning to the stack of crates. Deborah was in an odd pose, two arms tucked behind her back and two on her hips as she leaned forward slightly.

Mishikantz snorted again, rising to its feet with a low grumble. It was a couple of feet taller than Taren and easily three times as wide. Every inch of its body jiggled as it plodded around to the front of the desk, the stone groaning angrily as it leaned on it and looked us over again.

Its skin glistened with each movement, a thick layer of sweat coating its skin and the pungent aroma amplifying now that it was closer to us.

"That is more than usual," Mishikantz said.

"Yes. At least a year's worth. This will be my last haul for a while," Taren replied. Deborah clicked quietly behind us, her head slowly scanning the room.

"That does not work for me. I will require a delivery of this size every half cycle."

"You seem to be under the impression that I am one of your employees," Taren said carefully. "I do this as I see fit. This will be my last delivery."

Mishikantz let out a bellowing, smacking laugh that echoed off the walls of the massive room and made me feel sick to my stomach. *Really wish I had stayed in the hotel.*

It would have been wise.

That's not comforting.

Apologies. Something is not right.

What?

I am not sure. My readings of the room are being disrupted.

"Do you think you actually get these on the station because you are that good?" Mishikantz asked, letting out that disgusting laugh again.

"Yes?"

"You get them on here because I allow it. I tell the station to turn a blind eye. Only because you make me a lot of credits. No other reasons. I do not even like you, Taren Lulart."

"Yeah, the feeling is mutual, Mishikantz. Now, are you going to pay me so we can leave?"

"Here is what we are going to do," Mishikantz said, snapping a thick finger.

Six Purveyors stepped from behind the massive black pillars, each of them with a grin on their face and a weapon in their hand. Taren's hands dove into his coat, pulling out his gun, and I grabbed my own quickly, leveling it at a random target in the room.

I glanced over my shoulder at Deborah, to see what she had planned. She had hunched down, blades slipping from the wrists of two of her hands and a gun in another.

"Watch out!" I shouted as a seventh Purveyor slipped out from behind a pillar and slid a massive glowing blade through the air.

My stomach did a flip and my heart felt like it was going to explode in my chest as it pounded wildly. I was too late. The blade connected with Deborah's neck, severing it cleanly. It toppled to the floor with a loud clang as her body crumpled into a limp pile.

"No, no, no." I raised my gun and aimed it at the massive Purveyor coming up behind us. Taren's skin rippled, coating his body in stone as he readied for a fight, but didn't dare take his eyes off the others.

One of his arms wrapped around me, pulling me tight against him as he shifted us to a pillar, tucking me safely behind him.

"Drop it, Taren," Deborah's murderer said in a gravelly voice, holding the glowing blade to his side while aiming a long gun at Taren. The same voice that was over the intercom back at the grocery store.

"Grund. I had a suspicion you were involved on the other planet," Taren replied coolly.

"The other planet," Grund chuckled. "We know where it is now. No need to be secretive."

"You sent them to follow me." Taren maneuvered his gun to face Mishikantz as I did my best to look under his arm at what was going on.

I still had my gun gripped tightly and was ready to act when he did. My blood was boiling for Deborah, and I was ready to get revenge.

"Of course. Did you think you could keep it a secret forever? I grew tired of having to rely on you for the bananas. Now, these fine specimens are actually my employees and will deliver bananas on my schedule. I had hoped to keep you on. You are effective, but it seems we are at an impasse now."

"Wait, wait," Taren said quickly, holding his gun up before setting it on the floor slowly. "Drop your gun," he whispered to me, and I hesitantly set mine down. "Let us go. You can keep the bananas and you will never see us again."

"I will let you go. If you are seen on QT-314

or Earth again, I will torture you for three cycles before personally executing you," Mishikantz replied off-handedly.

"Deal, let's go," Taren said, grabbing my hand and pulling me to the door.

"No, no. You misunderstand. You may go, Taren Lulart. The human stays." My blood ran cold at Mishikantz's words. I can't imagine many reasons he would want me that don't end in me being forced to touch his disgusting body.

"She's not a human, she's a…"

"Enough," Mishikantz cut Taren off. "She stays. I have always desired a human. I can have all I want now that I know where they come from."

"No, that's…" Taren grunted with frustration as Mishikantz cut him off again.

"Taren, you have been delivering to me for several cycles now. Do not let anyone say I am not charitable," Mishikantz said boisterously, raising its arms and sweeping the room with them.

The Purveyors all nodded in agreement, never taking their eyes or weapons off of us as Mishikantz continued, "I will give you a hundred thousand credits for the human and two hundred thousand for the bananas. You will fuck off to the furthest reaches of the galaxy. It is a win-win."

A hundred thousand? Those Vlarkan were rip-

*ping Taren off. Still a little hurtful that a stack of ba-
nanas is worth more than me.* I would have found it
more amusing, but I was completely terrified.

I caught sight of Deborah's blank face lying
on the floor several feet from her body. My body
trembled as I stood behind Taren. But not out of
terror, out of rage.

"We should just kill him now," Grund said,
stepping closer to us.

"Now what kind of message would that
send about me?" Mishikantz replied, its mouth
stretching into a smile that filled its face from
side to side, revealing several rows of jagged teeth.
"Three hundred thousand credits, and you leave
with your life."

"Fine," Taren said, my heart sinking before I
remembered what he told me earlier about selling
me. *He has a plan. Thank you, whoever is listening.*
A sigh of relief escaped my lips, and I tensed up as
Taren stepped to the side and revealed me to the
room. "Money up front."

"Not an issue. Retrain him," Mishikantz said
suddenly.

"What?" Taren tried to move, but Grund
was on him in a flash, slamming a metal rod onto
his wrist.

The rod extended rapidly, spiraling around

his wrists and pulling them tightly together as Grund forced him to his knees and the bindings wrapped around his ankles. *Please tell me this is part of the plan.*

"Oh, ho, ho," Grund chuckled. "Someone's pissed." He grabbed Taren's chin and looked into his eyes. I glimpsed Taren's blood-red eyes as he trembled with fury on his knees.

CHAPTER FOURTEEN
TAREN

Blysh, this was not part of the plan. My body trembled and rippled as I seethed on the floor. The bindings around my wrist were too sturdy for me to break free from, not that there was much I could do with Grund standing over me. *I hate Nurans.*

All the Purveyors were Nurans from my planet. Scavengers that did nothing on their own. They only waited for someone else to do what they needed, then swooped in and took the spoils.

Mishikantz came towards me, each plodding step echoing in the silent room, its labored breathing growing louder and louder as it approached. Damp, icy fingers wrapped around my wrists, lifting them in the air as it passed a pad over my arm.

The display on my wrist popped up and showed a successful transfer of three hundred thousand credits before Mishikantz flung my arms down and lumbered past me towards Abigail.

Fire, hatred, and rage built inside of my hazy mind as I looked around frantically for any way out of my bindings. I had to protect Abigail.

The Call of the Vreth blazed to life again and ate away at me, almost causing pain as it tried to push me to protect her.

"No, stay away from me," Abigail said, darting under Mishikantz's grasp and rushing to me. She tugged at my bindings frantically, ignoring Grund approaching behind her. "Taren, what do we do? What do we do?" she asked, staring into my eyes.

My mind was too far gone to reply. All I could think about was killing everyone in the room and saving her as I strained against my bindings.

Grund snatched Abigail up as she flailed wildly, trying to break his grip. He was far too strong and held her helplessly in front of him as Mishikantz approached.

Mishikantz ran a thick, wet hand into the hood of Abigail's cloak, pulling it down and burying his hand in her hair. It let out a moan and said, "Ah yes. You will do nicely." Its finger trailed further down Abigail's face, caressing her neck. "Take her to my quarters," it said, motioning to a large metal door on the other side of the room.

"No, let me go!" Abigail shouted as Grund took her away. He let out a yelp of pain, dropping Abigail to the floor. She immediately scrambled away as Grund turned around, the thermal-blade buried hilt deep in his thigh. His gun came out instantly and he aimed a shot at her. A blue wave of light burst from the end, colliding with Abigail's back and flooring her.

Abigail's eyes were wide as her body twitched. The electrical impulses of the wave paralyzed her, a favorite weapon of the Nurans.

Heat built inside of me. My body felt as if a temperature greater than any star would consume it if I did not do something.

Every nerve inside of me was firing, screaming at me to act, but I was bound and could do nothing but glare angrily.

Mishikantz let out a laugh. "I like when they have some fight. You will be a treat." It walked past me, its stench washing across me as it slowly approached Abigail's twitching body. "I think I will sample you like this first, though."

My mind went blank suddenly. All thought left my head, and I felt completely at peace for a brief second, closing my eyes.

When I opened them, the fog that had been hanging over my mind was gone. The Call of the

Vreth had been fulfilled several hours ago and finally released me from its bindings.

I was free of the prison my biology had confined me in. Free to do as I pleased.

I had never felt more clear-headed in my entire life.

Never felt so sure. Never felt so right. I wanted Abigail. I needed her. It was not just the call. It was my own desire. She was the one that I needed in my life. She was the one that would make me whole.

Time slowed around me, as I watched the scene in front of me calmly.

Heat built faster and faster inside of me.

I should have been worried I was going to immolate, but I did not care.

All that mattered was saving Abigail.

My love, my heart, my mate.

ABIGAIL

Please, just move. No matter how I tried

to move, scream, or struggle, my body was completely unresponsive. I was helpless.

Mishikantz's hand reached toward me, coming within inches of my chest. Its eyes were all wide and focused on me, thick drool running from the corner of its grinning mouth.

A bright red light flashed behind Mishikantz's blubbery body, so bright it temporarily turned it into a black silhouette. It stood up as quickly as something its size could, spinning to face the light before lumbering hastily toward the door behind its desk.

Taren was there. Standing tall, his body coated in blackened stone, flames flickering from the joints. He stared at me, eyes burning embers that erupted into an inferno as he turned his sight to Grund. *Yes! Fuck them up, Taren!*

Taren raised a single arm, pointing it directly at Grund. Liquid metal dripped from his wrist, sizzling on the floor as it splashed onto the ground.

Grund and the other Purveyors immediately opened fire on Taren, his body disappearing in a vibrant display of green and blue light, only his black outline visible in the explosive display. Hissing sounded from all around the room as their guns released jets of steam and stopped firing.

The thud of Taren's footsteps was so heavy

and loud, I could have sworn the floor was shaking. He moved fluidly and with purpose toward Grund.

Taren's arm thrust to his side and a sword of black stone formed from his palm. When he closed his fist, the blade erupted into white fire.

Grund brought his blade up, the blue light surrounding it catching Taren's sword in the air as it came crashing down towards his head. The blue light flickered wildly before flashing red and the sound of breaking glass echoed off the black pillars.

The blue light vanished and Taren's fiery sword cut through Grund's with no resistance, hitting him in the shoulder and continuing across his body. Flames exploded from Grund's clothing along the charred black line Taren left, and he collapsed to the floor in two pieces.

The other Purveyors quickly weighed their options and rushed toward the door Mishikantz had disappeared into, Taren blocking the other exit.

They banged on it frantically as it didn't open, pleading with Mishikantz to let them in. If I hadn't been paralyzed, I would have smiled at the display before me. *Serves them right for killing Deborah and trying to rape me.*

Taren walked toward them slowly, leaving

charred footprints on the floor with each step, his sword at his side. The blade slid across Mishi-kantz's desk as he passed, leaving a black smoking line across its length.

One purveyor turned around and raised their gun at Taren, but it was far too late and Taren was much too close. His sword sliced through the gun, severing it in half.

The tubes connecting the handle to the barrel flailed wildly in the air, spouting green steam into the air. The Purveyor moved to throw the gun away from him as it hissed and let out a high-pitched squeal, but Taren clasped it, pushing it against the Purveyor's chest and staring into his eyes as he forced him into the center of the group.

The other five Purveyors started to run, but an ear-splitting, blinding, green explosion enveloped the group before they could take more than a step.

Blood splattered across the room, staining the white floors.

All that was left was a thick cloud of black smoke, green electricity spidering across it sporadically.

"Taren?" I squeaked out, slowly regaining control of my body. "Taren!" I fidgeted on the floor and bent my wrists. *Okay, come on, keep going. I have to help.*

A loud thud actually shook the floor, and a burst of air cleared the smoke. Taren was standing in front of the collapsed doorway, still clasping his sword and staring back at me. The flames on his body had diminished and his eyes were those smoldering embers again.

"I'm okay," I shouted, sitting up. "I think," I added, rubbing the spots of blood that had splashed onto my skin and cloak.

Taren nodded, turning toward the open doorway as the flames on his body burst into a frenzy again.

"Can we talk about this?" Mishikantz asked in the distance.

Taren remained silent and stepped through the doorway.

"Five hundred thousand. Six. Seven. A million. Ten million," Mishikantz pleaded. "Fine, have it your way."

A shrill alarm sounded, and a burst of green light illuminated Mishikantz's room. I wished I could move enough to look through the doorway.

Mishikantz's shouts turned to screams before being replaced by a loud squelching noise and the sound of flowing liquid. *Maybe it's best if I don't see.*

My heart froze when the door to the foyer

opened and the six station guards from the foyer rushed in, weapons at the ready. I made myself as small as I could and watched them, unmoving.

They all stopped in their tracks as the one in front raised a fist. Her presence was imposing, as she towered above the rest, and her armor barely contained the bulging muscles that coated her entire blue body.

I wanted to shout a warning to Taren, but I still felt weak and not fully in control. If the guards turned their sights on me, I wouldn't be able to do anything but die.

She crept forward, looking around the gruesome display with disgust, and peeked into Mishikantz's room as the squelching continued from inside.

She spun around quickly and rushed back across the room, a hand over her mouth and motioning for the guards to leave.

None of them hesitated and they immediately left, closing the door behind them. *Definitely best if I don't see.*

Silence suddenly fell across the room, save the crackling fire still burning on Grund. Footsteps echoed from Mishikantz's room, and Taren appeared in the doorway.

The sword was gone. His skin had returned

to normal, and his eyes flashed to purple as he approached me.

"Are you okay?" Taren asked, crouching in front of me and placing his warm hands on my shoulder.

The heat was soothing and made me feel calmer than I should have been. My life had flashed before my eyes and I thought I was going to be trapped servicing that disgusting blob for the rest of my life, but Taren saved me... again.

"I'm fine," I said, bursting into tears immediately. Taren pulled me into him and held me tightly.

The feeling of his skin against my cheek only amplified what I was feeling, and I cried even harder. So many emotions were welling up inside of me, and not just from what had happened.

I had fallen hard for Taren and even in the middle of all this chaos, it still made me sad he was only doing all of this because he had to. I wanted him to want me because he cared for me, not because he had to.

After sobbing for several minutes, I tried to sniff but ended up snorting and giggling, then crying again.

"Everything's okay," Taren whispered, squeezing me before pushing me away from him and looking at me. His gaze flitted down his own body before returning to my eyes. "I am naked."

"Yes, yes you are," I said, stifling a sob and giggling. "What do we do now?"

"Take our money and bananas. Deborah had another interested buyer. She always has a back up plan."

Taren grunted and stood up, offering me his hand, pulling me to my feet. I felt shaky, but Taren kept me steady as we walked across the room.

Deborah. Everything that had just happened was a blur, and I still felt disoriented from the deluge of emotions my mind had gone through.

So much so that I forgot about Deborah. I felt horrible and the back of my eyes burned as I stared down at her severed head.

"I can't believe she's gone… just like that," I whispered, crouching down and picking up her head.

"Huh?"

"What do you mean 'huh?' Deborah's dead. Does that not bother you?" I asked, glaring at Taren for a second before softening my stare. He had just gone through a lot, too, and was probably still processing.

"She's fine."

"Her head is in my hands right now, Taren," I replied, trying to keep calm.

"Yeah, that happens a lot. Come on," Taren said, picking up Deborah's body and placing it on the cart with the bananas. "Bring that with you."

Hope welled inside of me as I stared at her head in my hands and walked with Taren into the foyer. The guards were still out there, but they conveniently found something else to look at as we passed by, which was an impressive feat, considering Taren was completely nude and showing no shame as he strutted through the room.

Plus, he just killed their employer.

"Ah, blysh," Taren muttered, pausing to stare at Deborah's body on the cart. "Forgot a hand. Wait here."

Before I could argue, he disappeared back into the other room, leaving me alone in the foyer with half a dozen armed guards and Deborah's severed head.

All six of the guards looked at me as soon as Taren left, each one shifting uncomfortably when I glanced at them.

"So, what happened?" I looked for the source of the voice and found a green, four-armed man not much taller than me with his head cocked.

"Everyone is dead. I told you," a woman chimed in. The same one that witnessed whatever Taren had done to Mishikantz. "Keep quiet."

"Should we not... you know... capture them?"

"No."

"But we..."

"No. Silence."

"It is our job."

"Our job is to make sure no one comes in uninvited. They were invited in."

"But..."

"No more."

"Shut the fuck up Darynd," another woman added, her voice gravelly but still pleasant. She shifted her feet when I looked at her and I felt strangely empowered by that massive alien being nervous around me.

Taren returned, waving Deborah's severed hand at me like he was waving hello before tossing it on the cart.

"Ready to go?" he asked nonchalantly, like we were at a dinner party and it was getting late.

"Yes?" I replied, unable to hide my smile. "Are you going to do anything about that?" I motioned toward his exposed cock.

"I probably should," Taren said, looking around the foyer.

It was at that moment that it truly sunk in how perfect Taren was for me. As he scoured the room, completely naked and uncaring about the guards watching him nervously.

He let me make my own decisions and never forced me to do anything I didn't want. Thinking about it made me feel silly.

Oh, how little I ask of someone.

That wasn't all there was to it, though. Taren was there to pick me up when I stumbled, and he had a charming and sarcastic personality buried under his hulking exterior.

Maybe it wouldn't be so bad if we just ended up being friends. He offered me a place on his ship as a crewmember, so he has to like me in some way besides the bond.

I let out a heavy sigh as Taren fiddled with a door between two guards. A sharp pang stabbed at my heart at the thought of not being with him, and I fought back the tears brewing behind my eyes.

Two of the guards shrugged at each other as Taren disappeared into the side door. He reappeared a few seconds later, wearing one of those sheet robe hybrids that Mishikantz had on. It was far too large for even his huge stature and draped over him like a circus tent.

Taren held his arms out to the side and beamed at me. "New look. What do you think?"

"Please, no," I said, rolling my eyes and grinning with a heavy heart. *Truly perfect.*

CHAPTER FIFTEEN

ABIGAIL

Safely aboard the ship, Taren shrugged off the sheet/robe thing he stole from Mishikantz's, revealing his body to me again. I wasn't sure if it was aftershock, adrenaline still flowing, or what, but I couldn't keep my hands off him. He tried to go into his room to get dressed, but I corralled him into my room and into the shower.

"Do I smell that bad?" he asked, sniffing himself gingerly.

He didn't smell as good as he normally did. The smell of charred wood and ash still hung in the air around him, slowly dissipating as we made our way back to the ship. It actually wasn't bad, but I preferred his other aroma.

"No," I said, slipping off my own clothes slowly. Taren's face lit up when he put the pieces together, and his cock perked up. "They said Deborah would be ready in two hours, so we have some time to kill."

"Yes, we do," Taren said, slipping up to me and all but dragging me into the shower. I was having doubts about Taren and his real intentions, but at that moment, I didn't care. I just wanted to feel him against me.

It didn't go quite how I imagined. Once the hot water hit me, pure relaxation fell over me like a warm blanket and I got incredibly tired.

All the insanity we had gone through finally caught up to my body and mind, and I felt like I was going to collapse at any moment. I still took my time lathering up Taren's body and enjoying his soapy skin against mine as I leaned on him in the shower.

His cock took advantage of our proximity and slipperiness by rubbing along my thigh, but it didn't try to plunge between my legs like it normally did. *He must be tired too.*

I giggled against Taren's chest, running a finger along the length of his shaft and enjoying the heat radiating off of it as it went rigid.

"I think I got a little too big for my britches," I yawned before rinsing off the soap.

"What?"

"I fully intended to," I paused. "Well, fuck you, but I'm too worn out. The trauma today has been a little much."

Taren's cock fell limp between his legs almost instantly. "Me too," he replied with a yawn of his own. "I was fighting it and trying to keep my viln ready for you."

"How about a nap, then after…?"

"Works for me."

A burst of warm air billowed in the sealed shower, and the water evaporated from my skin quickly. I giggled at myself in the mirror as we passed. My hair was wild.

Taren and I climbed into bed together, both nude with promises of getting to business as soon as we woke up. I nestled under the blankets, pressing against Taren firmly before his heat started making me sweat.

I struggled to find a balance, eventually leaving my back exposed to the air.

"Much better," I whispered, nuzzling against him and feeling sleep already taking its hold.

"I need to invest in thermal-regulating bedding," Taren mused.

"Is that what they had in the hotel?" I didn't

remember getting this hot under the covers with him there.

"Yes."

"Definitely then," I replied, kissing him lightly on the chest. "So, are you going to tell me about what happened?"

"When?"

"What do you mean 'when?' At Mishi-kantz's. You didn't tell me you could turn into a lava monster, or make a sword appear out of your hand."

"You never asked," Taren chuckled.

"How am I supposed to know to ask that?"

I felt Taren shrug. "Can you turn into a lava monster?"

"No."

"Can you make a sword come out of your hand?"

I giggled. "No. I wish. I bet that feels weird."

"I could not tell. It felt natural, like extending a finger."

"Or your cock?"

"Yes. Or my cock."

"Is that like a thing that happens in puberty? You're sitting in your room, then suddenly a sword is in your hand and you're all embarrassed?"

"What is puberty?"

"Like… when you become a man?"

"Ah, vunlur. No, it is not like that. Although, my viln moving on its own was a bit of a shock."

"It didn't do that before?"

"When I was a sprout? No. One day I woke up, and it was moving. It was very alarming."

"Had you not seen porn or something?"

"I do not know what that is."

"Like… mating videos."

"Why would that be recorded?"

"You know what, never mind. That would be scary to wake up to. Similar thing happened to me as a kid, just more blood."

"What?"

"It doesn't matter," I yawned and tried to form another question, but it slipped my mind as I dozed off.

TAREN

I stayed beside Abigail for a while, watching her breath slowly as she slept. My central pilon pounded with each breath she took and I felt a strange ache of longing. She was so serene right now, so perfect. I wished I could stay in bed with her for the rest of my life.

She groaned in her sleep and turned over, revealing her naked ass to me. Her curves were immaculate, and I could not tear my eyes away for a few seconds, barely resisting the urge to rouse her from her sleep. It was insane to me how much I still desired her with the Call of the Vreth gone. I had hoped my feelings and desire for her would remain, but I did not expect them to stay so intensely.

I pulled myself away from the bed and went into the cargo bay, lowering the ramp and carrying one crate of bananas to the bottom. Plopping down on it, I watched the other people wandering the landing bay.

Most of them were going about their business like any other day. Rushing about and hurrying into the nearby district to sell their goods or get some much needed supplies. A few, though, were looking around starry-eyed and in disbelief at the size of the landing bay.

Newcomers, easy pickings for some of the more unsavory types on the station. While their faces were green, purple, covered in tentacles, spikes, or a few too many ears, they all had the same expressions.

Sheer wonder.

Just like Abigail had when we first arrived.

Another tinge of longing pulled inside of me and I released a heavy sigh, leaning forward and resting my elbows on my knees. I cupped my face with both hands and watched the people continue passing.

I never did that, but it was relaxing. Maybe I did need to slow down sometimes and enjoy the view. Abigail had suggested it, and Deborah frequently sat around and watched others. I think with Deborah it was more of an analyzing threats situation, but she did it either way.

My mind wandered, and I fell into an odd state of serenity. I was still more clear-headed than I ever had been.

The Call of the Vreth had released its hold on my mind, but I still felt the connection to Abigail. Me assuming my Vrethal form should have been hint enough at what was going on. The fabled Vreth-lock had taken hold of me.

The sword I had created was something only warriors of legend could do, and only when they had found their perfect mate.

I chuckled to myself quietly. If I had been on my home planet and done that, everyone would have been swarming to mate with me.

It was the sign of a powerful warrior, something that only a few were ever supposedly capable of doing, and none in the past two hundred cycles.

The Luranin women would have been all over me, but the joke of the entire thing is that in Vreth-lock you have no desire for anyone else but your mate. It differed from the Call of the Vreth, though. It was more real, like I actually was choosing this as opposed to being forced into it.

I chuckled again. Who knew I would ever be in this position, let alone be happy I was in it? It felt right to me, and for the first time in a while, I was actually happy.

"Hey, you!" someone shouted from nearby. I looked in the direction and saw a station guard approaching me.

Great. More trouble.

"Yes?" I replied, standing up and turning toward the guard. I towered over her and she looked more and more nervous the closer she got.

Her blue skin glistened in the light and

her white armor had pieces missing, revealing the shining flesh underneath. She held a stun-rod at her side, ready for action if I tried anything.

I knew what she was the instant I saw the wet blue skin. A Vulnir. Their skin is toxic to almost every species, but I knew why she was nervous. It had no effect on Luranins.

The guard looked me up and down before locking eyes with me and pointing her stun-rod at me. "No nudity on QT-314," she said sternly, waving the rod in the air to stress her point.

I glanced down and saw my viln dangling for all to see. "Blysh, I have had a bad habit of this recently," I said quickly, grabbing the crate and hauling it back up the ramp.

ABIGAIL

I felt a light panic when I woke up to an empty bed beside me, but it faded quickly and I rolled out of bed. My brain still felt foggy and like I could sleep for a good twelve more hours, but I was much better than I'd been earlier.

"Taren?" I called out as I checked the bathroom. *No sign of him there.* I left the room and started for the kitchen, but noticed the cargo bay door was still open and an orange light marked 'ramp down' was illuminated.

Slipping into the cargo bay, I saw Taren at the base of the ramp, heading back up with a crate on his shoulder. He was completely naked, and I laughed loudly as I went to help him. I chalked it up to his temperature regulation not alerting him he was cold, but it was still funny.

The second I stepped onto the ramp, a blue woman in station guard armor pointed her baton at me and shouted, "Hey! Like I just told him, no nudity on QT-314!"

My face burned hot as a cool breeze hit my skin and I rushed back into the cargo bay and up the stairs. Taren's cackling chased me the entire time. *Serves me right for laughing at him.*

"It seems we are having similar problems," Taren chuckled, placing the crate of bananas back in its pile before joining me at the top of the stairs.

"Apparently so," I said with a sheepish grin that faded quickly as Taren stared at me with his purple eyes.

"Is something wrong?" Taren asked carefully, stepping closer to me and placing his warm hands on my waist.

I planned on saying something cryptic like him and Deborah always did, and beating around the bush. I was never much for direct confrontation, but the promise I made to myself of not taking shit from anyone and rocking the boat all that I pleased echoed in my mind.

"The bond thing you had. I'm upset about it. I know you can't help it, but I really like you, Taren. A lot. It makes me sad to know that what I feel is real and what you felt is nothing but biology. The more I think about it, the worse it makes me feel." Tears burned at the back of my eyes and I tried to blink them away but only managed to let them fall down my cheek. "I want to stay with you. I want to be with you, and travel with you and Deborah, but I don't know…"

Taren opened his mouth to speak, but I continued.

"It's just that, miraculously, I can deal with the other worlds, the weird aliens, the unnecessary violence that seems to follow you around. The danger, the weird foods that are just gross. They're gross, Taren, you eat gross food." Taren shrugged and continued staring at me patiently, the shade of purple in his eyes deepening. "But I can't deal with not being with you. I don't know what to do, and I feel so alone in this and have no one to talk to about this. No advice to get. You can't even help me. You're just trapped in your bond thing and will probably do what I want anyway, and that's just not helpful. I could just…"

Taren's hand clamped across my mouth and I continued mumbling against it for a few seconds before falling silent and staring at him.

"The Call of the Vreth is gone, Abigail," Taren said, blinking slowly and stepping close enough for our bodies to touch lightly. His hand stayed firmly on my mouth as I tried to talk again. "I am free. My mind is my own. I desire you. I want to be with you. That is coming from my own wants, not from biological bindings."

I didn't know what to think or how to feel. Obviously, I was relieved and over the moon, but I had constructed this entire scenario in my head about how this would play out, and this was not what I had imagined. It was what I hoped, though.

"Really?" I mumbled against his hand.

"What?" Taren asked, moving his hand away from my mouth.

I put my arms around him and pulled our bodies together, letting the tears I had been holding back flow freely as I sobbed against him for the tenth time since we'd met.

"I do not understand," Taren said in confusion. His arms hovered just over me, and he moved them around as he tried to figure out what to do. He finally put them around me and held me tightly. "Why are you sad?"

"I'm not sad, dummy, I'm happy. I'm relieved," I giggled between sobs. "It feels like everything just fell into place perfectly."

"You make little sense."

"Why?"

"You are crying because you are happy?"

"It happens," I said with a grin, tilting my tear-stained face up to look at him.

Taren shook his head and smirked at me. "Humans."

I shook my head back at him. "Luranins."

"Well, what do you want to do now? We should wait for Deborah to return before we leave."

"I have some ideas," I said suggestively, taking his hand and leading him into the ship.

I drug him straight to my room and pushed him down on the bed. Both of us were already nude, so the mood transitioned much easier as I climbed on top of him and rubbed my hands along his rock-hard chest.

Everything that had been weighing heavily on my mind evaporated in an instance when he told me he wanted me and it wasn't because of the bond.

Once my mind allowed me to think again, all I could think of was having him inside of me.

Taren's hands immediately went to my hips and slowly slid up my side, leaving a wake of tingling. I shivered on top of him as goosebumps formed across my flesh and I giggled before leaning onto his chest and planting kisses as I worked my way up his body and to his neck.

Just before I slipped up out of reach, his cock slapped me on the ass gently, leaving a hot imprint, and I shimmied further up his body.

My lips found his, and I dug my fingers into his thick hair, gripping the base of his horn and running my fingers up its ridged shaft.

The feeling sent a ripple of heat through my body, and thoughts of his cock in my hand filled my brain as our tongues danced together.

Warm hands planted on my back as Taren pulled me tighter against him, pressing his lips firmly into mine as my own hands ran through his hair and across his horns greedily.

More tingling ran down my spine as his hands traveled up and down my back, each tingle shooting through me and straight to my core.

Heat built inside of me and it was amplified as Taren's hand slipped under my thigh and between my legs, finding my already throbbing clit and touching it just light enough to make me crave more.

Leaning back on him, I tucked my legs under his arms and reached behind me, grabbing hold of his cock and stroking it while his own hand worked its magic between my legs.

The sensations built and grew inside me while his cock grew harder and harder between my fingers, finally reaching its peak. My fingers slipped across the newly ridged surface and an insatiable pang of desire and hunger ravaged my mind.

I released his cock, and it swung itself back into my grip before I could pull away, so I granted it one last squeeze before adjusting myself and crouching just out of its reach.

Taren's hand immediately found its way back between my legs and his thumb ran up the length of my wet folds before pressing into my clit again and sending electrical chills through me with every movement.

Glancing down, I caught sight of his cock desperately reaching for the depths between my legs. *I wouldn't want to keep you waiting.* I grinned at Taren as we locked eyes, but he hit the perfect motion with his thumb. As I lost control, I closed my eyes and let out a quiet whimper.

Regaining my composure, I reached down

and gripped the base of his cock, lining it up and letting it slip inside of me. It clearly didn't need my help, as it wriggled its way inside of me the second it met my lips and I lowered myself onto it as it twisted inside of me.

I swore I could feel each ridge along its length as it slipped in and out of me, pouring its heat into my walls and causing my entire body to feel like it was throbbing.

Warmth surrounded one of my tits as Taren cupped it with his free hand, groping and massaging it and teasing my pebbled nipple as his thumb continued caressing my clit. The sensations became overwhelming, and I felt myself nearing the edge as pressure climbed inside of me to the point where I thought I would explode. Just as it became almost painful... release.

A groan escaped my lips as electric tremors wracked my body when I came. My breathing became shallow and frantic. It took all of my willpower to keep myself even remotely lucid, but I wasn't able to keep my balance and fell onto Taren's body.

His hand slipped out from between my legs and he wrapped his arms around me as he let out a groan of his own and his cock pulsed inside of me, filling me to the brim with his heat and sending me even further into the heated electric ecstasy that was consuming me from the inside.

I stayed on his chest, unmoving, with his cock inside of me as I tried to catch my breath. Finally calming myself, I rolled off of him, giggling as his cock slipped out of me and landed on his thigh with a wet splat.

I scooted closer to him and picked up his arm, pulling it around me and clasping it against my stomach with our fingers intertwined.

"That escalated quickly," I said with a grin, squeezing his hand.

"I was not sure what was happening at the beginning. You went from ranting, to crying, to more crying, to dragging me into the bedroom. I had a great time, though."

"I'm glad it turned out well for you," I giggled and nuzzled against his side.

"Do you feel better?"

"More than you could know."

CHAPTER SIXTEEN
ABIGAIL

"Right where you left it!"

Taren chuckled and pulled me onto his lap at the table. I had been trying to tell him goofy jokes that I enjoyed, but most of them apparently didn't translate, or he had no idea what I was talking about. I guess the legless cow was a hit.

Taren's laughter sounded a little forced, and I tilted my head up at him. "You don't get it, do you?"

"No," he admitted with a smile.

"Well, I tried."

"Let me try. What did the Gruthil do when it saw a Brethox pleg?"

My mind blanked at everything he said, and

I just looked at him expectantly.

Taren's face contorted into a smile and he could barely contain himself as he said, "It walked away."

Question marks danced in my brain and I suddenly understood how he felt when I talked about Spanish magicians and cows.

His face fell flat, and he added, "It's funnier if you read it."

"I'll take your word for it," I giggled, patting him on the chest and leaning against him.

"Hello," Deborah said nonchalantly as she stepped through the cargo bay door.

"Deborah!" I shouted, leaping to my feet and rushing up to her. Forgetting who I was dealing with exactly, I gave her a tight hug. To my surprise, all four of her arms wrapped around me and gave me a little squeeze. "I'm glad to see you're okay. I was worried."

"I told you it has happened many times before," Taren said, giving a nod to Deborah and leaning back in his chair.

"That was the third time. It has not happened many times."

"Yeah, if you say so. I feel like three times is a lot for being decapitated."

"I have to agree with Taren," I added with a grin.

Deborah clicked quietly behind her blank face, her head cocked at me. "I thought we were on the same team."

"I can be on both of your teams, right?"

"No," Deborah said simply, before changing the subject. "I scheduled a meeting for the other buyer on the way here, since we were behind schedule."

"That's fine. Where are we meeting them?" Taren asked.

"Here at the ship. They will arrive in ten minutes."

"That's convenient."

"Is it a good idea to let them know where we are?" I asked.

"It's not like we are permanently here. It's fine," Taren said with a shrug. "Less work for us. Speaking of work, come here." He motioned at Deborah.

She approached him, and he held up his wrist. Deborah placed hers above his and displays popped up as he transferred a hundred thousand credits over.

"A third of the bounty for you," Taren said,

then looked over at me. "We need to get you an AICC, then you will get your third."

"Really? A third? I didn't do anything really," I muttered.

"I will take part of her share if it makes her feel better," Deborah stated flatly, her head turning from me to Taren and back.

"Oh, um…"

"That was a joke," Deborah laughed. "You were present for the transaction and you will receive your share."

"Okay, thanks," I said with a smile.

"Besides, I was decapitated almost immediately and did little. I am not declining my share."

"Fair enough."

"Let's unload and prepare for the exchange," Taren said, jumping up and corralling me and Deborah to the cargo bay.

I mostly just watched as the two of them carried the crates down the ramp, and I tried to make myself useful by keeping watch. Several aliens passed by and each of them stared at the sleek crates, but thankfully no one approached.

Once everything was stacked and settled, the three of us sat on the crates and people watched. Deborah's blank face gave little indication of how she was feeling, but Taren looked re-laxed and almost like he was daydreaming. His gaze flitted from person to person, with occasional glances and warm smiles at me.

The two of them leapt to their feet before I even knew what was going on. Deborah bolted up the ramp of the ship and Taren moved over to me, gun drawn and head on a swivel.

"What's going on?" I asked, pulling my own gun from under my cloak and holding it at the ready. I really wasn't ready for more action, but I guess we don't have a choice.

My question was answered as I heard dozens of footsteps ringing on the metal platform below, growing louder by the second.

The footsteps sounded on each stairway at the corners of the landing pad, and the all too familiar white of the station guards appeared at the top of each staircase.

These looked much more capable than any of the others I had seen before. I could see it on their faces. They were hardened and well-trained, each one in much more advanced armor than I had seen so far.

Their weapons were complex looking, and they all moved with confidence and purpose, quickly surrounding the ramp leading to the cargo bay in a semicircle. There had to be at least twenty of them.

"Um, what do we do?" I whispered, nudging Taren gently.

"Nothing right now. Let's see what they want," he said without looking back at me, but I could hear the smirk in his voice. *Really wish I could stay that calm.*

Then remain calm.

Thanks, Deborah, that helps a lot.

You are welcome.

I have kind of missed this.

A thin, green lizard head popped up at the top of one set of stairs and continued to rise into the air as the creature made its way to the top.

It was incredibly lanky and looked like a strong breeze could topple it, but it towered above everyone else, easily twelve feet tall.

Its six arms were tucked neatly behind its back and something akin to a smile was on its face as it approached us. I wracked the information in my brain, but came up with nothing.

"Taren Lulart?" a velvety feminine voice asked. It took me a moment to realize that such a pleasant voice was coming from the lizard's face.

"Who's asking?" Taren replied nonchalantly.

"That must be you," the lizard smiled, stepping through the line of guards gracefully and crouching to be at eye level with Taren. "My name is Kelly."

"Seriously?" I blurted out. That was the first name I had heard that was even remotely similar to an Earth name. Besides Deborah, but I gave her that one.

Kelly's gaze switched to me and her mouth stretched into an open tooth grin, showing me every one of the hundred sharp teeth inside. "Yes. Who might you be?"

"I'm Abigail," I replied, steadying my nerves and standing up straight. *If I'm going to be a space pirate, I have to act the part.*

We are not pirates.

A slender hand came from behind her back with several very, very long talons. It reached toward me slowly, dipping into my hood and pushing it down. Kelly stood up quickly and let out a quiet gasp. "A human?"

"Yes?"

"Fascinating. Would you like to travel with me to Ethelox-12?"

"Um." I glanced at Taren as he shifted beside

me. "No, thanks?"

"Very well."

"What do you want?" Taren asked, his calm demeanor slipping away.

"The bananas."

"Deborah… or you may know her as DX-232zT worked out the details, but I am in charge. How much are you offering?"

"It was fortunate that we were in this quadrant," Kelly said, pacing in front of us with her arms tucked behind her back. My neck was already aching from looking up at her, but I continued following her as she moved. "We have been looking for you for quite a while."

"What for?" Taren asked. "If I wronged you, that does not narrow it down at all. I will need specifics."

Kelly chuckled and bent down to Taren's eye level again. "Oh, we were not looking for you specifically. Just whoever was smuggling bananas."

"Why? Do you want me to work for you?" Taren shifted in front of me. I could feel the heat radiating off of him as he geared up for a fight.

Kelly laughed melodically and said, "No. We want you to stop. We will take these bananas and you will cease all smuggling operations to and from the planet Earth."

"How do you know where Earth is?"

"We do not. Our employer is from there originally, and I am tasked with tracking down anyone who tries to manipulate the market."

"You are from ABs?"

"Correct."

"Blysh. I never thought you would catch up to me," Taren said stoically. "Well, this one's not involved." He motioned back at me. "She just got hired on here at the station, so let her go at least."

"Nope, I'm part of the crew, too. I've been with them the whole time. If you take him, you take me," I blurted out, not knowing what was coming over me.

I stepped beside Taren, not letting myself hide behind him. That was where I belonged, at Taren's side. No matter what, I'd stay there.

"How noble of you," Kelly said. Normally, that phrase would have been used sarcastically, but she seemed genuine in her tone. "You have two choices here. Be arrested and have your ship and cargo confiscated. We will take you to Ethelox-12 for trial and your punishment will fit the crime."

Kelly tilted her head and looked between the two of us.

"Or?" I asked, feeling much more confident

than I should have. Maybe some of Taren had rubbed off on me like I wanted.

"You cease smuggling bananas, relinquish your cargo, and go about your way."

"Deborah, stop!" Taren shouted.

I followed his gaze to Deborah, hunched over and creeping up behind the guards. She had long blades sticking out of two hands and a gun in a third.

All the guards and Kelly immediately snapped their attention to her.

Deborah stood upright, the blades disappearing with a quiet whir as she tucked her gun behind her back.

"Hello," she said cheerfully, pushing her way through the guards and standing next to me.

"You must be Deborah," Kelly said, much warmer than I'd have sounded if I caught someone trying to kill me.

"That is correct."

"A pleasure to meet you in person," Kelly replied before turning back to Taren. "Which option would you prefer?"

"How much are you paying for the bananas?" Taren asked. I immediately nudged him with my elbow. *We just got a ton of money, quit being greedy.*

Kelly chuckled. "You are a bold one. I like that in a man," she said in an unmistakable flirtatious tone that sent a slight pang of jealousy through me. "I have been authorized to provide you compensation in exchange for your cooperation. We will give you half of the market value."

"Full market value," Taren retorted quickly.

"Taren, just take it," I whispered.

"Half," Kelly replied calmly, staring into Taren's eyes with her head slightly tilted. She blinked slowly, her lids closing sideways.

"Seventy-five percent," Taren said.

"Half or nothing."

Taren opened his mouth to speak, and I quickly stretched my hand up to his face, planting my hand firmly across his mouth.

"Half is fine," I said. "We will take half and agree to your other terms."

Thick, hot, wet flesh caressed the palm of my hand repeatedly as I kept my hand over his mouth. I'd have chastised him for being immature, but who was I to say anything?

"Very well. Load the cargo up," Kelly said, pulling out a weird device and scanning the crates with a burst of green light before holding her wrist out to Taren as the guards gathered the crates and started hauling them down the stairs.

I pulled my hand away from Taren's mouth and my palm was all but soaked. Scowling at him, I wiped my hand off on the sleeve of his shirt, trying to ignore the warm feeling between my legs from the feeling of his tongue on my hand.

"I was going to agree to half," Taren said, shrugging at me and holding his wrist above Kelly's.

Three million credits transferred over and Taren's mouth fell open slightly, while my own eyes went wide. "Not to question a good thing, but I thought you said half."

"That is half of market value."

"Mishikantz was ripping us off," Taren mused. "I could have stopped a while ago."

"Well, I'm glad you didn't," I said, leaning up against him as he put an arm around my shoulder.

"Are you two not adorable?" Kelly cooed, still towering over us with a smile on her face. "Just like Alyssa and Drenas."

"They are adorable," Deborah chimed in, causing me to blush as I leaned against Taren.

We stayed in each other's arms as the last of the crates disappeared down the stairs. Kelly dipped her head to us and said, "If you are ever near Quadrant-63 stop by Ethelox-12. It would please Alyssa to see another human." She raised a hand to us and followed the last of the guards down the stairs.

"Well, that was intense," I said, letting out a heavy sigh. "It went much better than I thought it was going to."

Taren chuckled, and I smiled to myself as his body shifted against me. "Yes, much better than our previous deal."

"Isn't a quadrant only four parts? How is it Quadrant-63?" I asked.

Taren shrugged at me and I looked to Deborah for an answer, but she just approached Taren silently, holding her wrist out to him.

"Seriously? Not even going to celebrate first?" Taren asked with a grin.

"I have had my eye on some upgrades for several cycles and with this money I can afford them," she said flatly. "I am brimming with excitement and can barely control myself."

I giggled at Deborah. "You don't sound very excited."

"I am focusing on staying calm."

Taren placed his wrist over Deborah's and transferred a million credits over. I could actually see her trembling ever so slightly, and as soon as the transfer was done, she muttered a quick good-bye and bolted down the stairs.

"So, what do you want to do now?" I asked, peeking over the edge of the landing pad in time to see Deborah rush through the entrance to the station.

"We can do whatever we want," Taren said, slipping up behind me and wrapping his arms around me, pulling me tightly against him. "As long as I am with you, I will be happy."

I closed my eyes and pressed myself further against him, letting his heat seep into me and sighing deeply. "I'll be happy as long as you're there, too."

EPILOGUE
A Year Later

ABIGAIL

A green beam zipped across my head, colliding with the tree beside me and causing the purple bark to explode and shower across me.

"Blysh, that got in my eye," Taren said as we ran through the woods together.

"At least it didn't hit us," I chuckled, shifting the heavy backpack on my shoulder.

"Here is good."

We stopped in a small clearing in the dense trees. Taren slipped behind a large boulder and dropped his pack. It thudded loudly, and the contents rattled inside. I hunched down beside him, slipping off my bag and setting it down a little gentler.

"Where did they go?" a gravelly voice shouted from the woods. Heavy thudding grew louder as our pursuers chased us. According to

Taren, these were the last three guards left, and then we were in the clear.

Taren held up his hand, the electro-pulse scrambler armed and ready. I nodded at him and peeked over the rock, holding up five fingers in front of Taren.

The purple snake creatures in gold armor slithered out of the woods and as they drew nearer, I counted down on my fingers. 5.. 4.. 3.. 2.. 1.. I closed my fist and Taren stood up quickly, launching the scrambler at the three guards.

It exploded in the air. Blue arcs of electricity danced wildly before zeroing in on the gold armor and embedding themselves deep in the snake people.

They convulsed wildly and dropped their weapons, slithering for the woods in jerky motions as they tried to escape. Just before they hit the trees, they collapsed.

"That should be it," Taren said with a grin. "When did we take the first down?"

"I don't know, thirty minutes?"

"So at least an hour before any of them wake up. Should we go back for more?"

"Deborah is waiting. You know how she gets."

Taren grunted an acknowledgement before

scooping his bag up and putting it on. It was bulging and looked on the verge of falling apart.

Taren insisted that almost everything in
the temple we raided was valuable and crammed
his bag to the brim.

We walked into the woods, leaving the un-
conscious snake guards behind. I didn't envy the
massive headaches they'd have when they woke
up.

The trees gave way to a sweeping plain of
tall turquoise grass that waved in the breeze. Our
ships were sitting in a tight group, and Deborah
was busy rushing about them.

She was corralling the slaves we freed into
our two transport ships, while another Deborah
was loading up the plunder from our second trip to
the temple.

A third Deborah came out to meet us and
mercifully took my bag from me. I stretched my
arms and rubbed my shoulders, already daydreaming about the massage Taren was going to give me
later with his pre-heated hands.

"It's still weird seeing so many of you," I
mused as we climbed Virgal's ramp and into the
cargo bay to help Deborah load the crates.

"They are all me. I do not understand what
is weird about it," Deborah replied, taking Taren's

bag and rifling through the contents as another Deborah appeared from at the top of the stairs and rushed down the ramp.

"It's strange, Deborah," Taren said, backing me up. "But it's still convenient."

Taren stopped what he was doing and looked out of the ship before slowly walking down the ramp, stopping halfway and peering off into the distance.

"What's wrong?" I asked, moving over to him to see what was happening.

The turquoise grass stretched to the tree-line we had run from. The purple bark and green leaves of the trees all but sparkled in the light of the two suns, and the gleaming golden temple towered above even the tallest tree.

It was actually quite pretty.

"Nothing's wrong. Everything is perfect," Taren whispered. "It's hard to believe we are here now."

"What on this planet? You called it a… what was it… backwater…"

"Backwater planet with no hope of escaping the festering asshole of a pit they dug themselves into," Deborah offered helpfully, still unloading the bags into crates.

"Yeah, that," I giggled.

"No, not here specifically," Taren replied. "Here, in general." He waved his arms around.

"I know what you mean," I said, putting my arm around his waist. "I told you I was going to be Space Pirate Abigail."

Taren chuckled and let out a long sigh. "Free slaves, steal from the evil, give to the needy. You called it something else. Not pirate."

"Robin Hood! Robin Hood Abigail just doesn't sound as good. Plus, I don't think Robin Hood kept a share of his loot like we do. You know, Space Pirate Taren?"

Taren smiled at me, his eyes flickering to the deepest purple possible before he crouched down to my eye level and fished in his pockets.

"What are you doing?" I asked, feeling suddenly shy under his gaze.

Taren pulled a shimmering bracelet out of his pocket. It was a well-polished silver with dozens of black and red gemstones embedded deep into it. The one he stole back on QT-314 but cleaned up. He offered it to me, and I took it carefully from his hand.

"I love you, Abigail. You make me whole and have made me realize there is so much more to life than I ever imagined. I wish to be with you forever and I offer you my Vreth."

"What is it?" I asked, turning the pretty bracelet over in my hand.

"I have had it since I was born. Well, that's a lie. I had to steal it back from that shop I sold it to on QT-314. I never thought I would use it," he shrugged, then grinned widely. "But I am happy that I am using it. It's provided to Luranins at birth. If we ever meet our true mates, it signifies our connection."

"Are you proposing to me?" I asked, completely flabbergasted. Tears burned the back of my eyes as I held the Vreth with a shaky hand.

"If that means asking you to be with me for the rest of our lives. Yes."

I tried to speak, but couldn't get any words out, so I nodded wildly as I put the bracelet on my wrist. It was far too large and slid over my hand with ease, but as soon as I got it over my wrist, it tightened and adjusted itself to fit perfectly.

I threw my arms around Taren's neck and laughed while sobbing as I pulled his head against me.

"I love you so much," I sputtered out, squeezing him tighter and delicately avoiding slamming my head into his horns. "Yes. I'll take your Vreth."

END

Eager to see some Luranin women in action?
Mated to the Alien Captain *tells the story
of Idalas and Lily as they free a group of
slaves and team up with them to take
down the slavers while searching for their
HEA. Their motley crew is a wide variety
of species including three battle-hungry
Luranin women. Available on Amazon!*

*Curious about the human that started an
empire selling bananas and the tall lizard
people? Alyssa and Drenas have to fight to
survive against an evil, powerful being as
they navigate the perils of Ethelox-12 in* **Alien
Warrior's Bride**. *Available on Amazon!*

Printed in Great Britain
by Amazon